SHAE

ALSO BY MESHA MAREN

Perpetual West

Sugar Run

SHAE

A NOVEL BY

Mesha Maren

ALGONQUIN BOOKS
OF CHAPEL HILL   2024

Published by
ALGONQUIN BOOKS OF CHAPEL HILL
Post Office Box 2225
Chapel Hill, North Carolina 27515-2225

an imprint of Workman Publishing
a division of Hachette Book Group, Inc.
1290 Avenue of the Americas,
New York, NY 10104

The Algonquin Books of Chapel Hill name and logo are registered
trademarks of Hachette Book Group, Inc.

Printed in the United States of America.
Design by Steve Godwin.

The publisher is not responsible for websites (or their content) that are not
owned by the publisher.

This is a work of fiction. While, as in all fiction, the literary perceptions
and insights are based on experience, all names, characters, places, and
incidents either are products of the author's imagination or are used
fictitiously.

Cataloging-in-Publication Data for this title is available from the
Library of Congress.

10 9 8 7 6 5 4 3 2 1
First Edition

For M. R. O and G. G. M

Now if you don't hate me, beloved, don't love me.

—NICHARCHOS (FIRST CENTURY AD)

CONTENTS

1   Fireworks   1

2   Godstopper   25

3   Eva   41

4   Deep Vein   49

5   Kandice   62

6   Southern X-Posure   79

7   Honey Faker   97

8   G-LOC   115

9   Red Carpet   131

10   Flat Mountain   144

11   Terminal Lunch   157

12   Angel Bitch   166

13   Tamarack   173

14   Hammerhead   179

15   Crash n Bash   194

16   Count   202

Acknowledgments   209

SHAE

1 | FIREWORKS

We never have agreed on when we first met. Cam always said July, jungle gym, but I only ever saw August, bus hall.

I thought it meant something deeply bad, the fact that we don't remember it the same way. But sometimes now I picture Cam's version and it feels more real. I can smell the rain on the concrete and the way it fuzzes up the air, the heat turning the rain into steam. It smells like sulphur, too, out on the football field, sulphur and black powder, the ground charred from last night's fireworks.

In Cam's version, I imagine her ride down from Mingo after her mom's funeral, all the little tiny nothing towns and the twists and turns on Route 52. I can see her grandpa driving slow. At that rate it must've taken them all day to get to Greenbrier County. I can see Cam riding past my house before she knew me. I can see her looking at her grandpa's house, set up on the hill, covered in ivy and with those concrete steps climbing down.

I see her watching the fireworks out the front windows that night, the explosions shaking the thin panes. Or maybe she was standing on the porch.

I can see her coming across the field the next afternoon, the smell of explosives thick in her nose. I see her see me. Only it's not me yet. It's just a brown-haired girl on top of the jungle gym.

I went to school almost every day that summer with Mom, who was cooking for the free lunch program, making meals for the kids who were real poor with no food at home. I helped her prep, opening cans of pork and beans bigger than my own head, and then while they served them, I went out and read books on top of the jungle gym.

Cam claims that we talked that day but I can't see our conversation, not from my memory at least. I can hear our voices, sort of—Cam asking about the old brick high school where she thought she'd be enrolled in a month. Me telling her it was closed, telling her how they bussed us to Fairlea now. I can hear us but I can't see anything because I can't believe I could've seen Cam before that moment, that August, in bus hall.

I guess what I'm saying is I can't believe I could've seen her and forgotten.

In my version, I remember her walking into the Greenbrier East gym in her Tool T-shirt, head thrown back. Her shirt was long and baggy, almost to her knees, and under it she wore black off-brand JNCO-style jeans. Her blond hair reached her shoulders, and her nose and ears were pierced.

"Hey Mingo!" somebody called from the bleachers.

We were waiting for the evening busses. All of us Render kids on one side and the Frankford ones over on the other.

"Mingo's a vegetarian. He only ate french fries for lunch," Troy Baldwin called.

Cam already had a nickname. They were making fun, but even so it seemed special. No one had ever even noticed me enough to give me a nickname. Hey bookworm, somebody might say as they brushed past, knocking my book to the ground, but that was a general category, not really a name for me specifically.

"I know one kind of meat Mingo'll eat," Josh McCallister said, and everybody laughed and Cam turned and smiled.

Her teeth were shoved together in the front, but it only made her more beautiful. She shook her hair back from her face—almond-shaped eyes and cupid's-bow lips. The neck of her T-shirt was stretched and we could all see the delicate bones below her throat.

Maybe I've always called this my first memory because that day Cam was so shiny. When she talks about meeting me on the jungle gym, she sounds all wrinkled up, scared and confused. I don't guess I've ever been able to think of Cam that way. Scared and confused was me. I took up all that space. I needed Cam to be shining, always. I used to think that all I ever did was look at her. But maybe that's not true. Maybe I never did really see.

That day though, I watched Cam close. She got on the bus and kept moving past all the safer seats. She sat farther back than I was brave enough to go, so when Troy and Josh started in on her, I could only hear a few of the words. *Faggot. Pussy. Get that out of your ear.* When Troy climbed up over the seat, Mr. Kennesaw pulled the bus to a stop. He didn't call Troy or Josh's names. He took a clipboard down from his visor, studied it and hollered, "Cameron Burns."

Troy let Cam go and she stood up.

"Get off my bus," Kennesaw said.

Cam had a look on her face that was almost a smile. Her head thrown back again. She came up the aisle, bookbag dragging. She looked at me. I saw that her left earring was missing, and in its place, a bright stream of blood flowed down her neck.

In my version, that's our first look.

Kennesaw left Cam in that empty stretch past Davis Stuart Road, but she was in school again the next day and Josh and Troy were too busy flirting with Chrissie Hughes to bother her. Chrissie refused to sneeze, said it would mess with her makeup. She'd press on the tip of her nose and hold it in.

Josh and Troy kept telling her it was gonna come out as a fart instead.

In the evenings I usually got off at the elementary school to help Mom, but she was home with a cold that day, Cam's second day on the bus. After Dark Hollow Road it was only me and Cam left. I was Kennesaw's last stop.

"Burns," he called to Cam. "Get off here and walk up."

Outside was about ten degrees cooler than on that sweaty bus. The wind moved in the tops of the locust trees. Cam stood there, waiting to cross the road until Kennesaw backed the bus up. I kicked at the edge of the asphalt.

"You just moved here?" I said, looking up and then away, toward my parents' mailbox.

"Yeah," Cam said. "I live with my grandpa." And then she was gone, across the road and up the muddy track.

THAT EVENING I told Mom I didn't want to ride with her in the morning and help prep school breakfast. I told her I wanted to sleep in and take the bus straight to East.

"With how long that bus ride is, it'll only give you an extra half hour rest," she said.

I shrugged.

Later that night, on the phone with Daddy, she said, "Rodney, she's turning into a teenager."

I wouldn't help her in the cafeteria in the evenings anymore either. At first, I'd pictured that once I made Cam my friend, I'd go with her up to her grandpa's house after we got off the bus and I'd hang out there until Mom got home. But it turned out the other way around.

After the bus dropped us, I had nearly two hours before Mom got home, and I used that time to spy on Cam. We'd split right there where Kennesaw left us, beside my parents' mailbox. We'd nod at each other but never much more than that. Cam claims I was the one who wouldn't talk, that she tried to make friends all the way back in July, but I don't see it like that.

I would stash my backpack in my room and grab some Oreos. Mom always said she wished I would eat something better, but she still bought the junk food I asked for. I think she felt guilty about not cooking regular meals for me. Before I quit helping her prep, we would eat breakfast and supper together in the cafeteria every weekday. Breakfast was usually rushed, bites grabbed between tasks before I headed over to the high school. Supper was leftover lunch and we'd eat it out in the cafeteria after we'd scrubbed the school kitchen. We'd sit across from each other at one of those big long tables, the room echoing around us with the hum of the ventilation system. Mom would talk about which teacher had lost or gained weight and which one was having problems with her husband. Afterward we'd walk laps on the football field if the weather was nice and then drive home listening to the *Billboard* Hot 100 songs. Sometimes we'd hit the sale aisle at the Dollar General and buy a keychain with a heart-eyed cat or a lavender-scented hairbrush.

My interest in all of that had ended so abruptly it felt like whiplash. I didn't miss any of it but I almost wished I did. Instead, I had this new loneliness, wild and huge, and an endless desire to be near Cam. Of course, I didn't even know Cam, so she was whatever I invented in my head. My evenings with Mom in the cafeteria probably sound lonely but they weren't at all really. What was lonely was not wanting them and having nothing else instead.

It was probably gonna happen that year anyway, with or without Cam. But with Cam, I had something to call the pain wrecking around inside my brain. I listened to the Smiths' "There Is a Light that Never Goes Out" so many times that fall, it played even inside my dreams. I would put it on as soon as I got home, as I changed into my old sneakers, the ones I didn't mind wearing in the woods. I'd let it play twice more while I peed and picked at my face, leaning over Mom's hot roller set on the bathroom counter to get close to the mirror and inspect my pimples. This all gave Cam enough time to get inside her grandpa's house so she wouldn't notice me sneaking.

I'd cross the road and head up the embankment into the stand of white pines. When the weather was bad, the animals liked to shelter there, under the thick branches. I saw deer bedded down, and once a fox flashing between the dark trees. It was more than a half mile, but after the first time I knew how to shortcut diagonally and come out behind Cam's grandpa's woodshed. It was just pure luck that her bedroom was around back, facing the shed. If it'd been up front I wouldn't've had any cover. Truthfully, I couldn't see much though, light and shadow, sometimes the yellow of her hair, the shape of her movements as she crossed the room. Sometimes I heard her singing—sort of, maybe. I'd sit there and I'd smell pinesap and old wood and a dog scent, though Cam's grandpa didn't keep hounds. Then one day Cam's window opened and I spooked. I'd never considered that she could just open her window, and even though she couldn't see me, it changed everything and I didn't go back again.

Three days later she wore her Neurosis shirt.

"What's that?" I said, pointing at her chest as we got off the bus.

"A band," she said.

"Yeah," I said, "but like what?"

"What's the band like?" She tilted her head so that her hair fell away from her eyes.

I nodded.

"Like Tool if Tool was playing for God instead of for you."

"You're religious?" I said.

Cam laughed. "No like God in the bigger sense."

"Can I hear them?" I asked.

She held her phone up. "I don't have a plan. My grandpa won't pay for it," she said. "I can only use this when it's connected and my grandpa doesn't have internet."

"I do," I said. Our dial-up service was very very slow but I was desperate for this moment.

Cam followed me up the drive and I saw her see our house. A little brick bunker, gutters overflowing with reddish pine needles. It is so boring anybody would forget it the second they looked away, but Mom still talks about how much she loves it. Solid, snug, no drafts, no critters, no mold. I thought Cam's grandpa's house looked cool even with the windows on the second floor boarded over. But that was the kind of house Mom grew up in, a huge, once-fancy dump with wraparound porches and gables and all that. It would never hold the heat. She told me there was a hole in the floorboards of the bedroom she and her sister had shared and she used to stick her head in it and whisper all her sins: filthy thoughts and petty thefts and crushes. After she and Daddy got married, they lived in a trailer in Caldwell, but snakes had made a nest up under it. She'd come into the kitchen in the morning to get Daddy's breakfast ready and there'd be a black snake sleeping in the sink.

I led Cam in through the front door. I don't know why. Me and Mom always entered on the side that went straight into the kitchen, but for some reason it felt important to take Cam first through the sitting room with its picture window, china hutch, and cotton-ball lambs. The sun slanted so that it showed off all the dust on everything and it was super quiet inside, nothing but the sound of our feet wiping on the rag rug, the thud of the door closing.

"We'll have to use my mom's desktop. All we've got is dial-up," I said.

Cam didn't say anything.

Mom's computer was in the corner of the dining room/ kitchen, just past the eating table. Myrtle liked to sleep in the desk chair. She must've been almost fifteen then and she'd given up on cleaning herself. As I shooed her away, I could smell her old-cat scent and I realized that I couldn't remember the last time anybody besides me and Mom and Daddy had been inside our house.

I took the doily Mom had draped over the computer screen, and just as I was laying it beside the keyboard, I decided to put it on my head instead. I draped it so that it lay just above my eyes and turned to see what Cam would think. She smirked. I kept it there even when she looked away. We listened to the sound of the computer booting up slowly.

"Where are they from?" I asked.

"Who?"

"Neurosis."

"West Coast," Cam said. "Bay Area." She was look- ing at Daddy's framed certificates: Safest Driver 2016, Best Employee.

"How'd you know about them?"

"A forum."

"Then you went to a concert?"

She turned and looked back at me, eyebrows lifted. I took the doily off my head. "Your shirt," I said. "Is that where you bought it?"

"I ordered it," she said. "I've never seen them play."

I wanted her gone then. I'd imagined hanging out with her so many times and in my mind it was never ever this painful. I considered telling her the computer was broken, but I dialed for a connection instead. At least with music on, the silence might stop strangling me.

It always took more than a minute for a website to load. A site with music and videos could be more than five.

"You want some Oreos?" I got up from the computer and forced myself to turn and face Cam.

She shrugged. "Which one's your room?"

My room had two framed *Hunger Games* posters, piles and piles of books, a shelf of Calico Critters, and a purple chenille bedspread. It was spic-and-span clean.

"It's kinda messy right now," I said. "The sunporch is nicer."

Daddy had built the sunroom all along the back of the house for Mom to quilt in. Her sewing machine was at one end with a basket of cloth, and at the other, a glider and a broken elliptical. There were two doors that led to it. One from the dining room, one from my room. I took the Oreos out the dining room door and walked down toward the glider. I could hear Cam behind me, but when I turned, she had stopped and was standing beside the other door. The one that led to my room.

I sat down, hoping she'd join me. She grabbed the handle and turned. It was so bright on the sunporch and so dark in my room I knew it would take her a minute to see anything. If I got up and jerked her away though, it would only make things worse.

She stepped inside. My hand crushed the sleeve of Oreos.

I looked away into the back acre behind the house where the little Christmas tree Mom and I had planted was struggling, half its needles gone brown and sick.

"I was so happy they got Jennifer Lawrence to do Katniss." Cam's voice came out through my doorway. "Some people are born to act certain things."

Her face appeared, looking right at me.

I let out my breath.

And that's when the song drenched us. I had no idea what it was at first. A sound like a squeaky hinge but rhythmic. It wasn't until the guitar riff came in that I even realized it was music. Then the bass and drums surged. I had an automatic reaction to leap up and turn down the volume but Cam was smiling so big.

"A sun that never sets," she sang, "burns on."

She closed her eyes and her body swayed. I watched until I felt embarrassed, intruding. Even though she was there in my house, it felt wrong for me to watch her, more wrong than all the times I'd spied into her bedroom. I closed my eyes.

The music was more physical than anything I'd ever heard before. I understood immediately why Cam had said they were playing for God. There was so much pain and awe, and in its enormity it was beautiful, terrifying, holy.

We'd moved on to "Through Silver in Blood" when Mom got home. I heard her car pull up and I wanted to run to the computer and shut it off, not because she would punish me but because if she heard it then I would have to share this moment. But Cam was sitting between me and the computer, cross-legged on the floor, mouthing the words. I stayed where I was on the glider. I heard the sound of the kitchen door open, the jangle of it mixing with "Become the Ocean."

"Hello," Mom called, "Shae?" then more frantic. *"Shae?"*

Her face appeared in the sunroom doorway. "Oh, there you are." Her brown-gold eyes looked truly scared. "What is this?"

Before I could answer, Cam turned and stood. "Mrs. Phillips," she said.

I didn't even know she knew our last name and the fact of her knowing it produced a small stab of joy in me.

Cam smiled and said, "Is it too loud?"

Mom was watching her, lips slightly parted but silent, her eyes moving fast, taking Cam in.

Cam squeezed past her and I was shocked again. I didn't know anyone could have that kind of confidence, to move so freely inside a stranger's house. I thought for a second she was running away. Then the music stopped.

"Sorry about that, ma'am." Cam's voice sounded out from the dining room and then her body appeared in the doorway beside Mom. She held out her hand. "Cameron Burns," she said. "You can call me Cam."

Mom lifted her hand slowly. "Donna," she said.

"Nice to meet you ma'am."

Mom loves a "ma'am." If I were gonna psychoanalyze her I would say she spent her whole childhood waiting to be ma'am'ed. I'd say every time she ever used that word as a kid, she was jealous. Her whole face changed the moment that Cam "nice to meet you ma'am"'ed her.

"Chester Burns's grandson?" she said. "I've been meaning to drop by and see how you were getting settled. Now are you and Shae in the same grade?"

"I'm a year ahead," Cam said.

I still hadn't said a thing. Mom looked over at me. "Well, come on, Shae," she said. "I brought you chicken nuggets, unless you've already ruined your appetite." She looked back at Cam. "I'm so sorry, if I'd known you were here, I'd've brought more."

Cam shook her head. "No, that's okay, thank you ma'am but I gotta go."

I waited until she was gone to get up from the glider.

"Well, he seems nice," Mom said, setting a plate of chicken nuggets into the microwave. Ever since I quit helping her in the cafeteria in the evenings, she'd started bringing lunch leftovers home for both of us for supper. "But somebody needs to cut his hair and buy him some clothes that fit. I was worried when I heard Chester's grandson was coming to live with him. That man barely knows how to care for himself, let alone a child."

I sat down at the table.

Mom took my plate out of the microwave and set her own inside.

"Is he the reason you quit coming to school with me?" She looked up, and there was a twinkle in her eye that I wanted to squish, strangle, snuff. "You been hanging out with him every day?"

"No," I almost shouted. "Just today."

"Oh, okay." She walked to the fridge and came back with a nearly empty liter of Diet Coke. "I was trying to call you and get you to look and see if we were out of Coke but the line was busy the whole time. What's that you all were listening to?"

"Religious music."

Her forehead wrinkled. "Satanism?"

"No, Christian rock," I said.

CAM CAME TO my house three more times that week, and at first I thought she was just there to use the internet, which she did use—Facebook and the forums and all that—but she really seemed more than anything to want to share her music with me. When we'd made it through all the Neurosis albums, she played me Wolves in the Throne Room, which was more fury than Neurosis, more building, pulsing intensity. We'd turn the speakers to face the sunroom and crank it up. Cam liked to sit or lay while she listened and on the third day I joined her, letting my head rest three feet from hers on the yellow carpet.

Mom started bringing extra leftovers home and then she started talking about cooking us real suppers.

"Now what does Chester feed you?" she asked. "I can't imagine he cooks much."

"Groundhog," Cam said.

Mom laughed. Cam made Mom laugh a lot, which made me realize how little she usually laughed. "No, come on," she said.

Cam shrugged. "Well, sometimes he'll serve possum, too."

"Quit it."

She grinned. "Okay, more like Cheez Whiz and baloney."

AT THE BEGINNING of the next week Mom convinced Cam to ride with us to school.

"Now you know you don't have to stand out there waiting," she said. "I can give you a ride and you can catch the bus down at the elementary. It's only gonna get colder and I hate to think about you and Shae out there waitin'."

Cam agreed. I was seized up with something like envy. That was it, now our mornings of waiting together and afternoons in the house alone were all gone. I was too angry to say anything. The next morning Mom drove her Cutlass up the rutted lane to Cam's grandpa's house, and when it came into view, all tall windows and splintering wood, she tapped her horn lightly.

"Gosh, it must be cold in there," she said.

Cam stumbled down the steps and piled into the back seat. I didn't even turn to look at her. She had traded our time together for a free ride like it was nothing.

It wasn't three weeks later that she'd convinced Mom to let us use the car. She had her temporary license. She told Mom we'd all drive together and help prep breakfast and then she'd drive me up to the high school and we'd come back and help out again after three. No more bus. And it wasn't a month after that, she'd convinced Mom to get me a cellphone and put her on our family plan, too. Daddy already had one and it was only a matter of adding lines.

I think Mom was happy to have our routine disrupted. I think maybe she was just as bored of it as I was, though I never would've guessed. Cam turned our afternoons in the cafeteria into a party, Shania's "That Don't Impress Me Much" blaring across the kitchen while we mopped. With our phones and data plans we could listen to music anytime and it made my whole life start to feel like a movie.

Mom liked to take a nap when we got back to the house, so Cam and I would go out on the sunporch and listen through earbuds. But I didn't want to be separated and I was comfortable enough then to say what I was thinking.

"The music's better when we share it," I said and she agreed. At first, we each took one bud, but we couldn't get the full effect that way, so the next week I used my allowance to buy a splitter we could both plug into.

"The blood that flows through me is not my own," Neurosis crooned.

We had to lay close for the buds to reach. Both of us on our backs on the yellow carpet. When Cam rolled over to adjust the volume, our shoulders touched. I could smell her sweat, a sweet stink. I could feel her heat through the flimsy fabric of her T-shirt, washed so many times it was almost transparent. If I lost myself in the music, I could forget about my own body but never hers. Her nipples showed through her shirt, her pulse visible in the dip of her throat. And then one afternoon, listening to Isis's "In Fiction," she grabbed my hand, twisted her fingers in with my own and left them there.

BY THE TIME Cam met Daddy, Daddy had already heard so much about her. I was surprised when Daddy didn't say anything mean about Cam's hair or clothes, but Mom had already told him. Also, maybe Cam's look helped in a way. Daddy didn't think as much about what it meant for Cam to be hanging out with his daughter all the time.

It was awkward but it was always kinda awkward when Daddy was home. He only made it home two, sometimes three, times a month. Mom and I would count down the days but then it was like stuttering when he finally showed up. I remember that night Cam met him, we had spaghetti for supper. Daddy liked to have the TV on while we ate. I don't remember what we watched. I just remember that we had that New York Bakery brand garlic-bread Texas toast, the kind Mom only bought on holidays.

"Your granddaddy still got that GMC?" Daddy asked.

We all looked up.

"Uh, yeah," Cam said.

"I hadn't seen him driving it lately."

"He's working on it, I guess."

Daddy nodded. "The body might rust some but a small-block V8 like that'll keep humming."

Mom pushed the plate of bread away from herself. I could hear Myrtle scratching around in her litter box in the bathroom. Daddy wiped his plate with a piece of bread, put it in his mouth, and stood up. He walked down the hall and then walked back. He had a hammer in his hand. He crouched in the doorway to the living room and slammed it into the little metal track that edged the carpet and the linoleum. With each blow the ladle in the saucepot on the table bounced.

"Been meaning to do that," he said, "before somebody trips."

THAT FALL THE weather was funny. It got real cold in September, but in October it warmed back up. I almost want to blame that weather for everything that happened next.

One afternoon, Cam said she was taking the car to the river. We were at lunch together and she told me she was skipping class and driving down to the river.

"Wanna come?" She stood up to dump her tray.

The sun was so strong it was almost too much. We rolled the windows down and Cam drove slow. The trees had all changed their leaves in September, but when the weather turned they'd quit falling, and now they clung to the ends of the branches in fragile, hopeful husks.

The water was moving fast and very clear that day. We parked down by the bridge in Ronceverte, where we could see the island park with its summertime grills and picnic benches. Cam got out and walked around to the back seat. All the windows were down and Cam ran her phone's music through the car stereo. We didn't do drugs then, not even cigarettes. Cam's choice of course was more of a straight-edge thing, she'd already done a bunch of stuff by then and quit. Mine was just a serious lack of exposure. I wasn't cool enough to have had anyone offer me anything.

Cam lay down across the back seat and closed her eyes. I sat there listening to Amenra and under it the river, car tires passing, and the wind in the trees.

"My mom used to talk about this park," Cam said. "She told me she played softball here and in the summer they'd have a rubber ducky race."

I knew her mom was dead but I didn't know much else. Overdose, my mom had whispered, so sad. I'd forgotten that she grew up here and went to the same school we did.

"Do you miss her?" I said.

I heard Cam shift around in the back seat. "I missed her even before she was dead."

I let her words travel out the open window.

"I miss the her that taught me how to make an omelet and hospital corners on the bed."

Cam was quiet for a while and then she said, "By the time I was ten it was me begging her to eat but there wasn't never food in the house unless I brought it there."

I pictured Cam folding up half her school lunch in a napkin for her mom. She'd been taking care of herself for so long by the time I met her. The way she could smile and act all easy around adults, strangers even, I hadn't understood it until she talked about her mom and I realized then it was her most essential survival skill. From the moment I was born, I'd been given everything I could dream of and then some. It didn't matter that we weren't rich, my whole life had been one big, soft bed. I could climb in under the blankets and hide my head and everything would be okay. Cam had to smile her spectacular smile and show people that they wanted to love her, show them that they didn't want harm to come her way.

I knew I should say something to her. I knew it even then. Fear, I felt, ugly, awkward self-doubt. Cam had opened up and I stayed closed away. I should've even just asked her mom's name. But I didn't say anything. I thought I'd let the river say it for me. And then after a while I lowered my seat back until it almost touched Cam. She rolled over.

"Come back here with me," she said.

I moved slowly, like I was carrying something extremely precarious, some perfect balance I could easily upset. I opened the front passenger door and stood, warm wind all around me, lifting the hem of my shirt. I turned, closed the door quietly, and reached for the back handle without looking. I knew Cam's feet would be there when I opened it, black sneakers with knotted shoestrings, floppy pant legs, but I was not looking. I was watching the water, the way the leaves would fall and catch there, skittering and bobbing before they swept downstream.

She grabbed me and pulled me in. The music was as much a part of her embrace as anything, as if she'd planned it that way, timed it to the crescendo.

Her lips were softer than I had imagined. Under them I could feel her teeth and the muscle of her tongue. The music was gone, the river, the wind, the sun. I'd never focused so completely on any one thing. Cam's hands pressed into the skin of my stomach, my hips. I didn't know what to do with my hands so I put them on her chest, on top of her T-shirt.

After a little while she sat up. "Time to go get Donna," she said.

WE STARTED SKIPPING every day and instead of going to the river we'd go back to my house. There were no neighbors close enough to rat on us. We'd turn the computer speakers all the way up and take our clothes off, the afternoon heat in the sunroom drugging us into slow, lazy sex. The first time I saw Cam entirely naked it felt painful. I had to pace myself, if I took in too much of her at once, I'd never recover. Something so much bigger than my ordinary reality. I loved her long, loose limbs and the surprising plumpness of her ass.

I could not believe she desired me. I moved awkwardly, kept as much clothing on as possible. Gave her every chance to change her mind.

Afterward, we curled up together and slept.

By the time the weather turned cold I was probably already pregnant, though I wouldn't know it for a while yet. Mom invited Cam to stay the night for the first time after we'd watched Mom's favorite movie, *How to Make an American Quilt*. That was the beginning of Cam moving in with us, but we'd spent so many afternoons in bed together, it almost seemed like she already lived there. Mom said she hated to think of Cam walking up the lane in the dark, she said she knew it must be cold in that house. It was one thing if Chester wanted to live like that but his grandson shouldn't have to suffer. She made a bed for Cam on the couch. I lay in my room and listened to the pine branches on the roof until she came to me and curled in warm.

The morning we bought the pregnancy test was the morning of the first real snow. I remember my puke like a brown bruise against the white parking lot. Cam drove to CVS before school without saying anything. We'd used condoms every time except for the first but still somehow she knew to know.

In the CVS bathroom my hands were shaking. I'd left Cam in the hallway. Before I could unwrap the test, I needed the shaking to stop. The fluorescent light was rushing all around me. I needed everything to slow down—not even just the pregnancy really but something bigger.

Daddy told me a story once about a trucker he knew. This guy was on a new road, way up in the mountains, and he calculated his weight wrong for the grade. He got about halfway down and his brakes were smoking. He was going way too fast. He saw an emergency ramp up ahead, steered his rig off into the sand and started to breathe again but either his truck was going too fast or they'd built the ramp wrong, anyway he went flying off over the end. Crazy thing is, he lived, but both his ankles snapped from pressing down so hard on the brakes.

2 | GODSTOPPER

The blue couch was ugly even before I ruined it. Mom got it at a church sale over in White Sulphur when I was probably ten or eleven. It looked like a piece of dollhouse furniture, all old-timey and covered in blue velvet. It honest-to-God took Mom's breath away when she saw it. She didn't have the fifty bucks there in her purse so she made me sit on it and shoo people away while she drove home and emptied out her change jar. I got sunburnt sitting there. My nose and cheeks peeled for weeks.

It smelled funny even before I barfed on it. Then of course it smelled even funnier after that. When I started doing the homebound schooling, I'd lay on it for six, seven, eight hours a day. Cam and Mom were good to me, loading up the coffee table every morning with saltines and ginger ale and Gatorade. I'd have the TV on *The View* just to show them both I was gonna be okay and Mom would holler *honey, don't watch that all day, you gotta do some of those worksheets, too.* I'd turn it off before they even left the drive. Honestly, watching daytime TV all by myself just made me ten times more lonely.

In the mornings the light came in through the fake stained glass in the front door and the picture window. When it snowed, the pine branches held it in layers that dropped as the sun hit each one. I'd lay there and listen to them slough off like big sighs. And the little birds chittering and screeching. I had a bucket for barfing in but I tried hard not to use it too much cause then I'd have to get up and go empty it or lay there with the stink. When I felt my stomach bunching, I'd look up at the ceiling and focus on the water stain that looked like a miniature diving board. I made up a story about a girl who was famous for diving but she never could learn how to swim so every time she dove, somebody had to come save her.

If my stomach kept at it, I'd turn and grip the couch arm and concentrate on the carved wood. There were grooves dug into it that wound around and around in long curlicues. I'd trace them with my finger and make-pretend that they were roads to a secret kingdom. If you didn't know anything, they looked like a maze, like you'd never make it anywhere, but if you knew the secret, they'd lead you to a land of endless blue fields, soft and rich and ready for harvest. And out beyond the fields there was a river that ran dark and fast through the trees. Nobody knew where it went and mostly nobody ever asked because nobody wanted to leave. Sometimes I'd stand on the bank where the moss grew heavy and I'd watch it rip by and wonder if it could carry my body all the way to the sea.

When the sunbeams quit reaching through the windows that meant it was noon or twelve thirty. The sun was straight up above and I was more than halfway through my waiting. If the queasiness was gone, I'd do my worksheets. They were stupid easy. I mean, I don't know, but I wondered sometimes if they just gave all us homebound kids the same worksheets no matter what grade we were. The only good thing that came out of homebound schooling was when Ms. Lightner gave me *Wuthering Heights* and *My Ántonia* to read. I didn't tell anybody the work was too easy. I didn't tell anybody anything. I let everybody else speak.

I was stupid and afraid. I couldn't even tell Mom I was pregnant. I made Cam do it. That was maybe a week after the pregnancy test and I'd barfed all over the blue couch and we tried to clean it up but Mom found us and she took my temperature and put me in bed. I had the electric blanket up over my head and I was sweating like crazy but I wouldn't come out. *Tell her, you gotta tell her*, I said.

But I got what was coming to me when Mom made me tell Daddy, with Cam sitting right there, too. Daddy's face changed so fast and it looked like it would never change back, except it did, once Eva was born and he held her. I thought he might kill Cam. No, that's not true. I thought he might hurt Cam so bad that she'd never wanna come back. Daddy didn't even let me finish my sentence before he grabbed Cam, hauled her up. Mom took hold of me. I wouldn't quit screaming at Daddy until Mom got me in the bathroom and put me under the shower with all my clothes and shoes still on.

I don't know what all Daddy said or did to Cam. I do know I didn't see her for weeks, didn't see her in school, didn't see her at all. I do know I barfed my brains out in the nurse's office every day until finally they told Mom I ought to switch to homebound. And then it was almost Christmas and Mom walked in the door with Cam behind her, carrying a real tree. We watched *WALL-E* that night, the three of us huddled up on the blue couch, and when it was over Cam put her hand on my belly and said, "Let's name her Eva."

WHENEVER THE SUNLIGHT came through the back porch and on into the living room, that meant it was almost three. I'd empty my barf bucket and lay real still and quiet. The light was long and liquid, jittering waves across the ceiling. There were bird songs, freight train rhythms, sometimes a helicopter overhead, and eventually, car tires in the drive.

Cam brought me presents almost every single day. Sometimes a box of cherry popsicles, a DVD, a stuffed bear. My pregnancy memories are those endless blue couch days, our clothes-swap afternoon and Cam's Pocahontas County show.

I didn't want to wear the maternity clothes Mom had bought me. A HANDLE WITH CARE shirt and a bunch of floral muumuus. It was March by then, still chilly but warming, and we had the door to the sunporch open to let the light into my room. Cam had pulled out every item of clothing that I owned and spread them around me on my bed.

"You can still fit in this." She folded a Mountaineers sweatshirt. "Hey, I've never seen you wear this, or this." She was holding up a black jean skirt and a stretchy leopard print one. Walmart sale table. I had never tried them on outside of my bedroom. Even before the pregnancy, my stomach had pooched out over the top.

"Well, I sure can't now." I kicked at a pile of jeans.

"Can I?" she said.

I looked up. "What?"

Cam was looking right at me, holding those skirts in her hands. "You can wear my band T-shirts," she said, "they're big enough, you won't have to use those muumuus. I'll let you borrow some and you can lend me these."

"Why?" I said. I felt like there was some kind of lag, like a slowly loading web page that I couldn't make sense of yet. Cam looked right at me and her face was light, almost smiling, but there was something serious there in her eyes. If I could, I'd go back and pause here. I'd zoom in and study all the pixels of her face until I knew what to say. But it's not a movie and I can't pause, the action just rolled on.

She lifted her T-shirt and unbuckled her belt, let her loose jeans fall around her ankles. Her legs were skinny and pale.

We hadn't had sex in months. Hadn't had sex since we told my parents about the pregnancy. I felt a heat spread between my legs. Cam walked over and closed the door to the sunroom, turned and picked up the black skirt. It hit her mid-thigh and cupped her ass real nice. She tucked her T-shirt into the top and turned once in the mirror. It looked great.

I should've said that. Should've made the words loud and filled the room with them. Cam's eyes were on me. I should've never looked away.

"What do you think?" she said.

I should've looked at her face but I stared at her legs instead. Impossibly long under that black fabric. My skirt on her body.

I should've told her of her beauty. I felt it. I saw it. But I couldn't find a single word to say. I didn't want to know anything new about her. I was afraid it would separate us, make too much space. I always saw the miracle of Cam loving me as an accident. If I said the wrong thing, she would realize her mistake.

When I remember it now, I catch on that phrase. *What do you think?* she asked, and I did not say a thing. That hem of black denim against her skin. The lamp light low: I'd thrown a doily over the bulb. There's her ass in the mirror. Her voice asking me. When I think about it now, I want to drag myself up off that bed, tilt my head back and grab my own face. I want to make myself make words for her.

I THINK CAM met Jonas around that same time, March or late February. Or at least that's the first time she mentioned him to me. She brought home new music, a band I'd never heard, Wilgefortis. "Where'd you get this?" I asked.

"Jonas," she said and she told me how Jonas wanted to start a band and had asked Cam if she could sing, or scream. I felt a jump of excitement, Cam deserved to be up on a stage, I could see her in a rockstar way even as we sat there together on the stained yellow carpet.

"You should practice here," I said. "Mom won't care. We'll tell her you're screaming about Jesus."

Cam laughed. "No, Jonas already has the amp and drums and everything set up at his dad's house."

She told me how Jonas was homeschooled his whole life up in Pocahontas County but then his senior year his hippie parents split up and his mom moved to Lewisburg and told him he had to go to public school. Cam said Jonas was the grandkid of some of the original back-to-the-landers, the ones who moved here in the early seventies, the ones who hid their money, the ones with old Subarus and dirty feet.

I first met Jonas at Easter. Him and Cam had a school break and Mom was over at her sister's place. Mom had made Easter baskets for me and Cam, and Jonas couldn't stop laughing at the toy chicks and plastic grass. He took the bunnies out of the baskets and set them up on the table like they were humping. He ate all the black jelly beans.

We sat together on the sunporch and listened to the new Drudkh album. I closed my eyes but I could still feel him there, an itch that made the moment less than perfect. He listened to the album just like we did, eyes closed, body soaking it in, but he took up space between me and Cam.

"Your baby's gonna be born with black metal in her veins," he said, pushing his hair behind his ear and glancing at me. My lips smiled before I could stop them.

Jonas had a drum kit and guitar and all that at his dad's house outside Marlinton and Cam started going there with him after school. I think it hurt Mom, too, but both of us tried hard not to show it. I was feeling less sick by then and I took to walking in the afternoons. I didn't want to be at the house when Mom came home without Cam. There's a bald up on the end of the mountain behind Cam's grandpa's place, scraggly wild blueberry bushes and yellow-orange grass. Depending on the weather, it was either the wild moors or the great plains. It didn't really look like the plains but if I lay down in the grasses and stared straight up, I could see Ántonia coming toward me, her skirts hitched, ready to kill any rattlesnake that might try to bite me. On misty afternoons, I talked with Heathcliff. I told him Catherine didn't deserve him, she'd never felt pain like his. He put his hand on my belly and Eva kicked.

One day when I was coming back down from the bald, I saw the roof of Cam's grandpa's house glint through the trees. I turned off the path and followed the glint through the beeches until the peeling white paint came into view. There was a back door. I'd never been inside but I knew her room was just to the right. I was fully prepared to tell her grandpa that Cam had sent me over to get something, but I don't even know if he was home. Cam's room was full up with early evening sunlight, warm rays across the tussled bed, and the dresser with drawers gaping, mostly empty. A dusty glass of water. A makeshift shelf with bricks and planks of wood. It smelled so strong like Cam that my breath hitched in my throat.

I started sneaking into that room almost every day. I'd lay on the bed and feel Eva move and I'd look at the world from how it must've looked to Cam when she laid there. I don't even think she was staying at her grandpa's place at all at that point. Sometimes she came home with Mom and stayed with us, a few nights a week when she didn't have band practice. I remember a couple times Jonas came over, too. Otherwise, Cam was staying at Jonas's place. Jonas's dad even paid her to work some, helping to package and ship those special guitar picks he made.

One day Cam's grandpa caught me. Up until then, I hadn't seen him. I'd hear his footsteps around the house, creaking the floorboards or opening doors, but I never did see him until one evening I stepped out of Cam's bedroom to leave and he was standing in the hallway, eyes trained to the ceiling. I looked up, too, and there was a blacksnake there, veined out across the top of the door. I looked back at him and he looked at me but he didn't say anything. I took off running.

I LIED. I do have one other memory before the Pocahontas show. It was my last ultrasound, in May. Cam came to every single appointment. And the one time I had a checkup and didn't tell her about it, she freaked out. *She's my baby, too.*

Eva was positioned wrong. She'd settled in butt first. We'd been working to try and move her for weeks. Cam massaged in circles on my pelvis and I tilted and rocked. We put ice packs up at the top of my belly where Eva's head was, to try and get her to turn away. Cam even pressed headphones against my skin, just above my panty line, and played Mozart, because some woman in Boston said her baby had turned that way, flipped out of breech just to get its head closer to chamber music.

I was already pretty sure Eva hadn't moved. She didn't feel any different in me. But Cam was real hopeful. The sonogram lady spread the jelly all across my skin. It was slick and cold. She started to move the probe and Cam leaned in. I could smell her, ChapStick and sweat. The lady made a *tsk* sound with her mouth.

"What do you see?" Cam said. "Did she move?"

The sonogram lady looked at Cam and I wanted to smack her. I hadn't liked the way she looked at Cam to begin with, the way she took in her long hair and earrings and torn T-shirt, but I especially didn't like it now that she was staring at her all pitiful.

"We did everything you all recommended," Cam said. Her blue eyes were huge. I focused on them because if I thought about anything else, I would feel it coming, a panic-dread running over me. Most days it felt like my pregnancy would never end, I couldn't imagine anything after. Sometimes, though, I looked up and saw it racing at me up the road: the terror of labor, my body flayed open.

THE POCAHONTAS SHOW was a sort of graduation celebration in place of walking. Cam and Jonas didn't want to do the caps and gowns and I'm sure I wouldn't've wanted to, either, if I could've. Walked, that is. But it wasn't my year and since I couldn't, I really wanted to, or wanted Cam and Jonas to.

Cam drove me up to Marlinton in Jonas's dad's Subaru that afternoon. I was feeling carsick by the time we hit Droop Mountain and she slowed, took the curves extra careful.

She rolled down the window and blew out her cigarette smoke.

"I'm gonna quit smoking the day Eva's born," she said.

I realized I didn't even know she'd started again.

Everything was new green. Fluorescent baby leaves on all the trees. I watched the roads and lanes slide by and wondered which one led to the place where those Rainbow Girls were murdered. I asked Cam if she knew and she said it was back by the Droop Mountain Battlefield. She said Jonas's dad knew the man who'd found their bodies—those two girls who'd hitched rides to a hippie festival and ended up shot in the head.

Jonas's dad's place was back off an unmarked dirt road. It was a whole compound of wooden buildings, some of them stitched together with tins roofs over walkways. Cam told me it was the last piece from what had been a big communal acreage back when Jonas's grandparents moved here.

Jonas's dad wasn't home but his sister, Shoshona, was. Cam left me with Shoshona while she and Jonas and the other band guys went to get set up. I couldn't tell how old Shoshona was at all. She looked like she wasn't much younger than me, she had tits already and everything, but she kinda talked like a baby. Actually, she wouldn't really talk to me at all. She had a bunch of little toy horses—tiny plastic mares and stallions— and she'd wrapped each one up in a piece of colorful cloth. She unwrapped them and stood them up on a log in the yard and talked to them, or maybe *for* them, I couldn't really tell.

The thing about all the back-to-the-land kids I've ever met is their crazy confidence. Even the super awkward homeschooled ones have this solid, bone-deep confidence. It's like their parents pump it straight into them while the rest of us just kinda fumble and doubt. I mean, Cam had a lot of sureness and she wasn't raised that way but hers felt earned, like she got knocked down so many times she didn't give a shit. Shoshona acted like respect was her birthright.

"Mayhap we shall try again next plowing season, m'lord," she said, holding a yellow stallion high against the bright clouds.

I wandered away. I was real pregnant by then, my belly heavy and clumsy and my back always aching. I could hear Cam and Jonas and the other band members in the backyard testing the microphones. I wandered into one of the sheds. It was so much darker inside, I couldn't see at all for a minute until slowly my eyes adjusted to the strips of light falling through the slat walls, honey-colored air full of dust that streaked across long planks of wood like nothing I'd ever seen, blond wood striped all crazy with black or swirled with reddish patterns. The moment I reached out to touch it, I heard footsteps behind me and I jumped.

"Tiger eye," the man said. "It's beautiful, isn't it?"

He was tall and skinny, with a braid that fell over his shoulder all the way to his thigh.

"Smell this." He bent and picked up a curled wood shaving and held it to my nose. I clasped my fingers under my belly and breathed in. It was a warm, rich smell.

"You're Shae," he said, letting the curl drop to the floor.

I'd already guessed he must be Jonas's dad. Eliot.

"Cam has told us so much about you. We're very excited for the birth," he said. His eyes oozed kindness but they made me squirm. Somehow hearing the word "birth" in his mouth and thinking about him thinking about me giving birth made me want to vomit. It felt way too personal, even though everybody everywhere seemed to want to make my pregnancy public—total strangers touching my belly at the grocery. "What are you having?" they said, "How many weeks?"

Eliot showed me to a hammock under a willow tree so I could get off my swollen feet. From there I could see the corner of the stage and some of Cam's band's flurried movements.

This was gonna be their first show and all of them walked with a thrill in their step. I could pick Cam out by watching her blond ponytail and her camo pants as she moved among them.

Eliot asked me if I needed anything and I said I'd like a Coke but he brought me a glass of water instead.

"It's best for the little one not to have too much sugar," he said.

His braid creeped me out, the way that he had knitted it all the way to the tiny end, the way that it brushed against me when he bent to give me the glass.

Once I'd gotten settled in that hammock I didn't want to move. Cam came by and checked on me a few times. I asked her if maybe they had iced tea and she brought me some, but it was bitter so I poured it out across the roots of the willow tree.

When the sun was touching the tops of the branches, people started arriving. Most of them I didn't know but some of them had been in my class. All of them pretended like there wasn't a pregnant girl in a Valdur shirt laid up in the middle of their party. Johnny, the drummer, built a fire not too far from where I was and people started cooking hot dogs and kebabs. Jonas came over with a rattlesnake he'd found dead on the road. He asked if I wanted some.

"Tastes like chicken," he said. "Just watch out for the little bones." He looked like a miniature version of his dad—not quite as tall and his braid wasn't as long, but otherwise just the same.

"I'll stick with hot dogs," I said.

It was dark by the time the band was ready to play, but Jonas had rigged up a whole network of stage lights: Christmas twinklers, glowing Halloween pumpkin bulbs, and colored spotlights. I heaved myself up from the hammock. My left foot had fallen asleep. I jiggled it real fast. I wanted to find Cam and wish her good luck or break a leg or I love you so much. But I didn't see her anywhere. The air was thick with weed smoke and campfire smell. I had to pee real real bad. I hadn't been inside yet and I couldn't even tell which building might have a toilet in it. So I was off in the bushes getting poison ivy when Cam came out on stage.

I was crouched just beyond the edge of the yard, clinging to a little sapling for balance, when all the lights went out and then just the stage ones came back, blinking. Jonas walked on and went over to his guitar, followed by Aaron, who picked up his bass, and then Johnny, who waved to the crowd and sat down behind the drum kit. They were all silent and I wondered with a jolt if something had happened to Cam. Then the lights quit blinking and a purple bulb streaked on over the microphone. Cam walked up out of the darkness and the first thing I saw was her legs: smooth and shining. Even from that distance I could tell they were shaved. And then my skirt, my black denim Walmart sale-table skirt. And a cut-off black T-shirt, crop-topped to show a strip of her white belly. And her hair was down, soft blond curls all around her face. Her eyes ringed and her lips rouged just a tiny bit.

There was a rush of sound like a wind through the crowd and then her voice rang out over all of us.

"Hey everybody we're the Godstoppers," she said and then she paused and I saw her eyes harden. "And I'm Cam," she drew her breath in, "and I'd like you all to know that my pronouns are she and her."

And then Jonas's guitar rose up and Johnny's drums lurched at us: one-two, one-two-three-four.

3 | EVA

It wasn't the poison ivy that made me have a C-section. I know that. Eva was stuck butt-first and then she came early. Still, it felt like I did it to myself.

I'd been soaking in oatmeal baths for days. I couldn't even put on panties. The itchy blisters spread all across my thighs and pussy. Cam and Mom wanted me to go to the doctor about it but I was way too embarrassed. We'd called the nurse hotline and the lady had said I would be fine. Eva would be fine.

The bathroom was under a pine tree and laying there in the tub I could hear the branches brushing on the roof. I had the window open and I could hear the birds, too, hopping and screaming. I gooped the cold oatmeal up onto my thighs. I squished it through my fingers and plastered it on my pussy and it was so gross and so ugly, I laughed and laughed, and when the itching rose up uncontrollable, I gripped my own arms in my hands and I pinched myself until the pain was worse than the itch.

Cam and Mom carried the TV in and strapped it onto the toilet so it wouldn't fall. Cam brought me ice cubes and I let them slide all over my thighs. Later, when I was in Jason Hicks's kitchenette in Ronceverte and that kid from Clifton Forge had OD'd and they were filling his pants with ice, packing it up around his balls, I remembered this. I remembered Cam bringing me tray after tray of ice and how she looked at me like she loved me even when I was so ugly and it made me hate her.

Over and over again in my head, I heard her saying *I'd like you all to know that my pronouns are she and her.* Her voice breathy but strong. It snagged in my brain and tore. *Her.* I have to admit that it took me a minute. It was so completely and immediately true but how could that be the first time that she mentioned it? I blinked and saw Cam up on that stage. Me, pissing in the poison ivy. I ripped through my memories like I was searching my bedroom, throwing things left and right, wanting to find the moment she had told me personally and privately. I'm not saying I never messed up Cam's pronouns, I know I did, but honestly right away it felt so obviously true. I just couldn't believe I hadn't known. I thought back to the skirts. That CD that she brought home back in February—Wilgefortis—the photo of the singer with her black hair and blood red lips. "I'm pretty sure this is the first black metal band to have a trans woman singer," Cam had said and looked at me. And I didn't say a goddamn thing.

I didn't say anything to Cam until after Eva was born, although I did start thinking *she*. I didn't say it. I said "Cam" or I talked around her. And neither of us said anything to Mom. Cam was transitioning right under her nose and Mom pretended like nothing was happening. She's good at that. And so am I. I don't know what Daddy thought, he's never been one to say much, but if I had to guess, I'd say he tried real hard not to think about Cam at all.

THE PAINS STARTED in the night. Six days after the show. The pain was tangled all up in a dream I was having. I was riding one of those mechanical horses they've got at the grocery store. The kind where you put a quarter in and it rocks you back and forth. I was riding one and I started to not feel too good. Then I started to feel real bad, shooting pains all through my belly. I looked around to get someone to help me but the grocery store was just full of empty buggies and the horse kept rocking.

I woke up and I knew right away something was different. This pain was coming from deep inside. The poison ivy pain was nothing compared to this. I called out Cam's name.

WHEN I THINK about everything that happened after that, the pieces always get a little mixed. I have some images and some facts but they don't all fit together real well. It's like one of those true crime shows where the evidence *almost* paints a picture that makes sense.

There's real facts from my charts like: breach positioning, cesarean delivery, lacerations, bladder flap, incidental cystotomy not recognized intraoperatively, postpartum hemorrhage, puerperal fever, sepsis.

And then there's memories. But they change every time I look at them:

It was real warm that night, and when Cam and Mom walked me to the car I could hear the peeper frogs going crazy in the creek at the bottom of the hill. We drove through Render and it started to rain. The pain would rise and shriek through me and then shrink back and I'd feel the poison ivy welts again. The windshield wipers went *flip-flip, flip-flip* and we slid under a yellow stoplight and the lights of the whole world were smeared like melting candy across the glass and I could see my body down below. I was already in a hearse, moving sleek through the dark night, and Cam and Mom were real sad and I felt bad for them. But not for me though. I was beautiful in the back of the hearse.

In the hospital it was too bright and too loud, clanging metal trays and rustling paper and everybody moving so fast. I felt the bite of the spinal and I screamed and then I could not move. Just my arms and hands flapping. I watched them jerk across my chest and I told them to quit but they would not stop.

The nurses strapped my arms down but they still wriggled rebelliously. The pain was gone but I could feel vomit coming up, up, and then it splashed out across my chin and neck. I could feel a burning tickle across my belly and then the doctor tugging inside me. He was yanking and pushing and moving my guts up and down.

The sheet was blocking half of me but I could see the look on Cam's face when things went bad.

"Eva," I said. "Eva?"

Cam nodded and kinda tried to smile.

The bottom of the sheet, where it met my skin, was darkening.

I heard Eva cry. A shrill bleat. A sharp bolt of leaping sound. My heart volted up with it and I could breathe! And I could see! Electric-pure-charged-energy. I looked at Cam's face. She nodded again but still wouldn't smile.

The nurses and doctors were talking some strange language, fast and low. Cam's eyes were huge and I noticed then that my whole body was shaking, buzzing and bucking like something vibrational had got all up under my skin.

The one nurse grabbed my hand, the one with the IV line. I guess that's when they put me all the way under. Nobody told me anything and I think I thought I was dying. But Cam was there, floating just above and beside me, all warm and gauzy yellow.

WHEN I WOKE UP, I was alone. I came back into myself from the corners. There were little bits of me stuck up there in the cardboard drop tiles and the light fixtures. When I'd gathered enough of myself, I opened my mouth. Nothing came out. My tongue was huge and dry and unmoving. I looked myself over. Everything seemed to be there. I was whole. And fat and stupid. There was one main sensation, a deep strip of pain in my belly. This was not like the pain before, this one was fixed and unchanging.

A nurse squeaked by with a fluttering clipboard. She stopped and looked back. Her face opened up.

"You're awake," she said.

"You left something in me," I said, surprised to hear my voice working.

"What's that sweetie?"

Maybe my voice only worked inside my head.

"I think you left something bad inside me," I tried again.

She laughed, repositioned her clipboard.

"You stitched it up inside me."

She smiled real wide. There was a smudge of pink lipstick on her front tooth.

For a moment I felt foolish. It was Eva inside me, of course, I thought. Eva inside me, hurting. I didn't see her anywhere in the room.

"Your incision's bothering you?" the nurse said.

"What?"

She set her clipboard on the table and came over and pulled down the sheet and pulled up my gown until my skin was all showing. All the roundness was deflated and I was wearing paper panties like a big diaper. At the top of the diaper was a row of black stitches. My heart went jagged when I saw it. She bent in to look close. Her hair smelled like vanilla frosting.

"I'll be right back," she said.

"Where's my baby?" I watched her pick up her clipboard. I was asking all the wrong questions. There was something there on the paperwork that I was supposed to know but I was too slow.

"She's in the nursery. I'll let them know you're awake," she said and left.

She'd covered me back up but I could still see the stitches in my mind. Black spider legs bunching the white flesh. I was afraid to move. My diaper was wet.

When she came back she had some pills in a Dixie cup.

"Where's my baby?" I said.

"For the pain." She held out the cup.

That was the first Oxy I ever took.

I didn't know anything, all I knew was before too long I didn't care that I didn't know. The questions weren't gone exactly, but now they had no fangs. The world was tender, cupped around me like hands around a tiny flame. And I had walked through a violence tall and deep as any midnight and I was here to say my own name.

That first time, there in the hospital, was the best Oxy I ever had, and since then I've always been just trying to get back. Back to that lush bruising, the petting warmth that spread and pulled Cam and Eva into that room.

Cam's hair was up in a high ponytail and the thing in her arms was our daughter. Cam's face, I'd never seen it like that. Shining, beaming heat. She climbed up into the bed and Eva was a seashell, tiny, pastel, perfect. So much of her curled: eensy fingers curled in fists, swirled curl of her ear. She had eyelashes. I felt them against my fingertips and the thrill sped through me all electrical.

"The nurse showed me how to help you get her to nurse," Cam said and her voice tugged me up toward the surface.

"What?"

"To latch on."

Eva's eyes roved under her closed lids whenever Cam spoke and my throat froze. Eva was already Cam's. And Cam wasn't mine anymore, if she ever was.

4 | DEEP VEIN

Eva's always been good. I mean, she cried some but it wouldn't be right if a baby didn't cry. Mostly she just seemed to sleep or nurse, pressing her tiny nose into my tit and working at it, her fists clenched and eyes closed.

Or maybe that's just how I remember the first two weeks cause of all the Oxy and the pain and the fact that there were so many people around to help out, I never had to just sit there with her crying. Daddy took a week off and he met us at the hospital. He was giddy, wouldn't quit sniffing the top of Eva's head. And then when we got home Cam moved into Mom and Daddy's house and far as I know there wasn't any fuss about it. Mom even put a dresser on the sunporch for her things. School was out and Mom was just cooking for the summer lunch program so she only had to go in for a couple of hours. Otherwise, we were all there in the house. I don't know what kind of truce Cam and Daddy made. Mostly they just seemed to ignore each other. Eva was the focus.

My days went in a big circle that had three parts. In all of the parts there was the pain that ran like a belt through my belly, sometimes more, sometimes less, depending on the Oxy. I told everyone the pain wasn't coming from the stitches, but no one would believe me. I mean I think they believed I was in pain but they didn't believe it was coming from inside me. When the doctor figured out that they'd cut my bladder and then left me with an infected gash, they felt bad. But for those first ten days or so everybody just kept saying it'd get better.

WHEN THE OXY kicked in, it did get better. The throbbing was still there but faded now and the love around me rose up bright and new. We were all together there in that little house tucked under the pine trees with all our love pouring out of each of us and into Eva. We passed her around and stared into her face. We laughed and lowered our eyes. Her beauty made us all embarrassed.

When the Oxy really kicked in good, I'd drift and sleep. And when I woke, I wouldn't know, for a moment, what my life was. When I woke, I'd feel the pain, anchored in my middle, while everything else bobbed just out of reach. It was like waking inside a flooded house with all my belongings floating around me, pieces of my life I could barely make out. My baby there in Daddy's arms, Cam and Mom in the kitchen singing. When I surfaced more, the pain rushed in. I was bleeding all the time, thick, dark, red, all over my thighs all day long, it leaked out of my diaper while I slept.

I couldn't take a bath for fear of infection, which I already had but we didn't know it yet. Mom would hold on to me through the shower curtain, her sitting on the toilet, propping me up, telling me school gossip from the cafeteria. Blood running down my legs and over the chipped green nail polish on my big toe.

Mom wanted me to walk. She was scared of something called deep vein thrombosis. Blood clots that formed after abdominal surgery and rose to your lungs and heart and killed you. Walking was preventative. I couldn't walk. On the day she made me go down to the mailbox with her, I passed out. Little spring flowers growing in the ditches, tiny blue-and-white blossoms, little yellow coltsfoot. I stared at the flowers and at Mom, she was yelling for help. She touched my forehead, slimy with sweat, and after Daddy got me up out of the ditch and into the house, she took my temperature. 104.

After that's when they did the second surgery, to fix my bladder and get rid of the sepsis. I was in the hospital for four more days. Cam and Eva came to visit I think but I can't remember exactly, it all blends in, the first time in the hospital and the second. I do know the second time around they sent me home with a catheter and a brand-new bottle of Oxy.

WE LAID UP in my bed together, Cam, Eva, me and my catheter bag. I hated to ask Cam to help me, but Daddy had gone back to work and Mom was down at school during the middle of the day. Jonas's dad had gotten Cam a job at the health food store in Lewisburg, but Mom made her wait to start it until I had my catheter out and me and Eva could go up there with her while Mom worked. Mom was afraid to leave me alone with Eva.

It was disgusting and embarrassing. Who the fuck has a catheter at sixteen? They told me they hoped my bladder would heal completely and I wouldn't have to use it forever but I saw in their faces that they didn't know really. The ache was less now but I kept taking Oxys at the same rate. They helped me quit worrying about the catheter.

We watched Netflix all afternoon. "I need to go take a shower so I can't tell if I'm crying or not," BoJack Horseman said. I looked at Cam. The TV screen reflected in her eyes, squiggles and stars.

"Why didn't you tell me?" I said.

"Huh?"

"Your pronouns."

We hadn't talked about it at all yet.

"I did," Cam said, staring straight ahead.

"No," I said, "you didn't tell *me*, you told everybody."

She shrugged, still staring ahead. "I tried," she said. "Before then. You weren't listening."

I felt the room tip just a little. It was already too late. I knew she was talking about that day in my bedroom. Our eyes. Her body in my skirt. I should've said something.

I moved to face Cam, the blankets were scrunched up and Eva was sleeping in the crook of her arm.

"Did you think I'd have a problem with it?" I said. "It doesn't make any difference to me."

"It should," she said. "It's a big deal to me, so it should matter to you."

"I didn't say it didn't matter, I said—"

"Whatever."

Her face looked like it was underwater, the light of the TV moving liquid all over it, her hair fanned out across the pillow. She was more girly now but it was subtle, she wore the same JNCO knockoffs and T-shirts but she washed her hair every day and wore it down all the time and her eyes were outlined, her lips a bit pink. How did she know she could do it? Be that brave. I couldn't imagine what it would take. Her strength shimmered all over her, breathtaking. I wanted to have even just a smidge of her bravery, enough to let me say "what next? What's your plan?" I was scared, too. I'd seen *Boys Don't Cry*. I was scared they'd take her. I was scared she'd leave me.

Cam sat up straighter in the bed and used her free hand to slide her cigarettes out of her pocket without disturbing Eva. I watched her wrestle with the pack with her one hand, trying to get a cigarette free. I focused in on her fingers. After a while, I reached over and took the pack and pulled one out. When I handed it to her, our fingers brushed and I felt a flicker.

She lit it and blew her smoke up and away from Eva, into the corner of the room. I needed to touch her again. We spent hours on the bed or the couch but I couldn't remember the last time I'd touched her on purpose, just because I wanted to feel her skin. When I thought about it, I felt like I was gonna cry, tears knotted up in my throat. I did not want to cry so I reached for her smoke. She looked at me like I was crazy. I'd never asked to bum one, never ever smoked before.

"You shouldn't," she said.

I grabbed her wrist, small and bony with her pulse jumping there under a snarl of old friendship bracelets and corded leather strips. "Fuck you," I said.

As soon as I inhaled, I started crying anyhow. Slow, quiet tears down my cheeks. When I passed the cigarette back, Cam noticed.

"Hey," she said and rested the cigarette in the ashtray between us and reached for my face. She rubbed the tears away with her thumb and said, "How's your catheter bag?"

THE NIGHT BEFORE Cam's first day of work, we all went to Walmart to get her new clothes. She wanted to go alone but I'd gotten my catheter out that day and was desperate to do something. Cam and Mom had to push me in a wheelchair around the store but I didn't care. I'd taken an Oxy just before we got in the car and fed Eva in the parking lot and I was blissed just to be out of the house, to watch the high-up lights in the ceiling all glowing and people walking and shopping, their voices bright around me.

While me and Mom and Eva were in the baby section, Cam split off and came back with an armful of black jeans and black T-shirts. Mom wanted her to buy khakis and polos but Cam pointed out that she was working in a hippie health food store.

"You could probably get a job at the Greenbrier," Mom said. "In one of those gift shops, or on the golf course maybe, or taking people's luggage up to their rooms."

Cam smiled and shook her head. "I need something that's real flexible," she said. "So I can start classes at New River in the fall."

That shut Mom up good.

At home, in our room, Cam showed me her clothes. Black knockoff Pumas, tiny black T-shirts, and black girls' skinny jeans. She looked real cute, the stretchy jeans cupped her ass and the tight T-shirt showed off her super-flat stomach. I felt a flash of fear. In her JNCOs and band T-shirts, she just looked androgynously alternative. In her Walmart outfit, she looked like a girl. I thought of the boys on the back of the school bus, the blood dripping from Cam's ear.

EDEN'S HEALTH FOOD STORE smelled warm. Nag Champa and sandalwood and about a billion herbs from all over the world. I nursed Eva in the basement with all the spices and herbs and while she sucked and cooed, I read their names to her. Herbs de Provence, cumin, mustard seed, garam masala, lavender, motherwort.

Cam got the hang of the register real fast and could make change quick and easy in her head and I was proud of her. I watched all the rich hippie ladies and how they looked at her and wanted to not like her with her too-dark, too-tight clothes but they couldn't help themselves. As soon as they talked to Cam, they started flirting, flinging their silk scarves around and asking her opinion on any old thing, just to have an excuse to stay at the counter with her. I hung around in the background, running my fingers over the essential oil bottles and packages of rice cakes. I was only there for a few hours every afternoon. Up until Cam and Jonas went halfies on a GMC van, Mom drove us everywhere. In the morning we'd all load in and drive Cam to work and then Mom and Eva and me would go home until it was time for Mom to work lunch and then she'd drive me back to Lewisburg so me and Eva wouldn't be alone. She came to get us when Eden's closed. Sometimes we'd all eat Shoney's buffet or burgers at Jim's Drive-in, but mostly we ate cafeteria lunch leftovers.

Once Cam and Jonas got the van, Cam could drive herself and Mom just had to drop me off and pick me up after her shift. Eden didn't seem to mind me being there.

Sometimes Jonas and the other bandmates came by the store and we'd all go out back into the alley for a smoke. I'd bum one off Aaron, and Cam would frown at me and

look at Eva and say, "Don't get smoke in her face." Jonas
had a girlfriend who started coming along, too. She had long
blond hair she wore in a fishtail, almost as long as Jonas's dad
Eliot's braid, and a beautiful juicy ass that confused me. Or
my body's reaction to her ass confused me. I almost felt nau-
seous as I watched it move under her thin cotton dress but I
couldn't stop watching. Cam caught me at it once and grinned
so big I busted out laughing and woke Eva up.

THE DAY BEN came into the store it must've been midsummer.
It was hot upstairs and I'd taken to napping in the basement
with Eva on a yoga mat somebody had left there, behind
the big bins of nutritional yeast. I was exhausted beyond
exhausted and Cam was, too. Eva had slept pretty good for
the first two and half months but then she'd taken to fussing
all night and sleeping during the day.

I woke on that purple mat, Eva drooling into my armpit
and the heavy funk of yeast in my nose. I heard Cam's voice
upstairs—chatty, excited—but I couldn't make out her words.
And then a man's voice answered her back. This went on for
a while but I didn't listen. I lay there and let my eyes unfocus
again. I wanted an Oxy but I'd left my bag upstairs. I wanted
a cold drink from one of those expensive tropical elixirs in
thick glass jars inside the cooler. Eva started fussing, rooting
around in my armpit for a nipple.

I stood up and cradled her, pulled my tank top down and
latched her on my tit and carried her toward the stairs. That's

when I realized Cam was still talking to the man, had been for a while now. I came up into the hazy brightness of that afternoon and saw Cam leaned over the counter and I saw Ben, though I didn't know to call him that then. I saw Ben in his collared shirt, laughing. And Cam's eyes, I saw something in Cam's eyes and her mouth—the way she was looking at Ben, something so alive I knew immediately I wanted to snuff it out. I stumbled and Eva lost her grip on my nipple and started screaming and Ben turned and saw me then, my tit hanging out, dripping milk onto Eva's face and onto my sneakers and onto the hardwood floor. I knew to hate him right away.

IT WASN'T THREE weeks later, Cam was going up to Charleston with Ben for an appointment with a hormone doctor he knew. The thing I've never been able to figure out is if Ben just happened to start coming into Eden's when I wasn't there or if he knew when Cam would be alone. That first afternoon, he'd turned away from the counter and I'd stuck my tit back in Eva's mouth and we all kinda shuffled around until he'd paid for his Altoids and left. I didn't see him again for weeks but Cam started talking about him a lot. Environmental lobbyist. Ivy League schools. She started spouting out random facts about water pollution and mine waste pools. I always thought of that one afternoon as the first time Cam met him but I don't guess that's probably true. He must have been dropping by Eden's to chat with her before that. I just only learned about him later through dribs and drabs of facts. Twenty-five years old. Fresh out of law school. Living in Charleston but traveling down to Lewisburg weekly to research a new case.

I would've gone to the hormone doctor with Cam. She'd gone to every pregnancy appointment with me and I figured that me and Eva would go along with her. But she said it was too much trouble to bring Eva and when I said that Mom could watch her, Cam straight up said no. It might confuse the doctor, she said. *I* might confuse the doctor.

I went to work with Mom that day and lay with Eva in the grass in the shady corner of the football field while Mom cooked. I made a tiny clover crown for Eva. I wished Cam was there to see it. Even though I'd carried Eva in my own body, literally made her from my flesh and blood, she seemed more and more like an extension of Cam, those blue eyes and blond curls. I thought about Cam at the doctor. I thought about how great she'd look with tits.

In a few weeks school was gonna be starting again and I knew Cam and Mom were trying to figure out what to do with me. Neither of them trusted me home alone with Eva. I'd never done anything to hurt her but I'd sleep so deep sometimes I didn't hear her scream. Sometimes I dreamt that I'd smothered her accidentally.

THE SECOND TIME I ever saw Ben was out front of Eden's. I was waiting for Mom, Eva hanging against my chest in a sling. Ben walked up, white shirt tucked into starched jeans.

"Shae," he said.

It took me a minute to remember his face, to understand why this man would say my name.

"Hey." I jiggled Eva to keep her asleep.

"How's it going? How's Eva?" The sun struck the peaks of gel in his hair.

I nodded, jiggled Eva. "She's sleeping."

"Cam's inside?"

I nodded.

"I was so happy to hear that the doctor finally approved her estrogen."

I looked down at Eva's head. My heart was beating dizzy and there was Ben, on the street, just talking about Cam's transition so openly. I was jealous of so many things about him but maybe most of all his conversational bravery. I snickered, or snarled, or something like that.

I was so full up with Oxy and jealousy. I wanted Cam's love like a bowie knife, a crazy gorge bridge with blood and veils. *For all eternity, until you and I die and die and die again.* I expected it all without saying a thing.

"You two met over at Greenbrier East, right?" Ben asked.

I nodded. All I could do was jiggle and nod.

"So you're starting college this fall, too?" His eyes beamed honest, clean paternal curiosity.

"I didn't graduate," I said.

The lights in his eyes turned down a notch. "Oh, of course, with Eva." He gestured at my chest. "But you'll catch back up."

There was a car horn beep behind him and I saw Mom's Cutlass pull up. Inside she was smiling, a purple sweatband wrapped around her head. I pushed past Ben and tried not to picture Cam's face, the way it would look when Ben walked in.

After my second surgery, Mom had gotten memberships for me and her at the SilverSneakers gym. It was all old people. Just my pace, she said. She told me exercise would help my body get rid of the pain. The only thing I was strong enough to do was walk slowly. I'd strap Eva on and we'd walk the track around the edge of the room every afternoon. The pain in my bladder was still there—less, but still there. I was scared there was something deep and forever wrong with me.

The track was an endless loop, but on the wall beside the water fountain there was a paper arrow and each day someone would turn it, left or right, just to spice things up.

"Oh look, sweetie," Mom said, her voice pitched up all bright. "It's a leftie day!"

5 | KANDICE

Kandice had a face like a black-and-white movie star. Clark Gable or Cary Grant. Strong cheekbones, soulful eyes, and a cleft chin. She kept her brown hair back in a low ponytail and wore a Kenny Rogers baseball cap all the time except when she was on stage. Of course, I didn't see her on stage for a long while, at first I didn't even know she worked at Southern X-Posure. She told Mom she worked nights at a telecommunication center and made calls to other parts of the world that were just beginning their days. Actually, that's what she told Juanita who worked with Mom, and Juanita told Mom who told me. Kandice needed a babysitter, not at night though, at night her three kids slept at her mom's place, she just needed somebody to watch them while she slept during the day.

There'd been a fire. Down at the teal HUD complex where Kandice lived. Turned out it was her four-year-old, Tasia. She'd lit the living room curtains one by one and Kandice hadn't noticed until the fire department came.

Mom thought it was perfect for me. *It'll get you and Eva out of the house a little and give you some cash besides*, she said. What she meant was that with Tasia and Sirena and Tony bouncing around, I was less liable to pass out.

Cam was starting classes at New River and Mom was back to her full-time cafeteria schedule. She'd drop me and Eva at Kandice's mom's house in the morning. Kandice's mom, Brenda, worked up at Tudor's in Lewisburg, and she'd be in the bathroom getting ready for work when I got there. Tony and Sirena were jerking on her legs while she tried to keep a steady enough hand to put on eyeliner.

"Mornin'," I'd say and haul them out of there to give her some privacy. Mom said for us to come over to school for breakfast, but I could never get them together in time; sometimes we'd go for lunch. If she could've, Mom would've kept us with her all day, except Kandice's kids didn't have car seats so she couldn't drive us all across town. Besides, the principal would've found out about it eventually and Mom couldn't afford to risk her job.

Tony was a little too old for the playpen but it took him a good ten minutes to figure out how to climb out of it, which usually gave me enough time to fix Tasia a bowl of cereal and change Sirena's diaper. As soon as Brenda left for work, I let them all scream and spill Cheerios across the linoleum while I lay and nursed Eva on the couch in the dark living room. Brenda's vacuum cleaner probably had three full boxes of Cheerios inside it.

I tried to wait till afternoon to take my second Oxy but sometimes I couldn't. The pills weren't working as well as they had at first and sometimes I had to double up. Sometimes the pain reached up through me like a rotten tooth, stuck right there inside me and it hurt so bad I couldn't even pick Eva up without crying, so I'd put everything I could find that might possibly somehow turn dangerous into a cardboard box on top of the fridge—pans and knives and lighters and curling irons and forks and batteries—and then I'd put on the *Winnie the Pooh* DVD. By the time I quit watching Kandice's kids, I had that whole thing memorized, Pooh's voice weaving in and out of my Oxy dreams. *Doing nothing often leads to the very best of something.*

ON TOP OF the hill outside of town, just overlooking Render, there's a big old cemetery. It took us almost two hours to get up there, me and Tasia together pulling the red wagon with Tony and Sirena inside. I kept Eva in a carrier on my chest.

"I'm *tarrrred*," Tasia would say, and she'd drop down in the grass along the sidewalk. I'd sit down, too, lay back and feel Eva wiggle against my chest. She was big enough now she wanted more than just my tit. Sometimes she wanted to look around and coo. I tied Sirena and Tony to the wagon so even if they jumped out they couldn't run in the road. Or if they did they'd have to drag the wagon with them.

When we made it to the cemetery they could run and run and run and run until they reached the end of the world and nothing could hurt them. Or that's what I thought, but they still figured out ways. I let Eva out of her carrier and she would roll in the grass with me and watch the bugs or the clouds. There was so much time. Time. Time. Time. Hanging off every tree and dripping down in great big stretches. I never ever knew the grown-up world held so much time. And I was in charge of all of it. When my watch finally said two, we'd go to Kandice's.

Kandice always had Dum-Dums suckers for each of the kids and a shot or a beer for me. The first time she handed me a shot of Jim Beam, I looked at her all funny.

"What?" she said. Her voice was a slow smoke rasp. "You're not pregnant anymore."

I'd never done a shot before. I swallowed it and coughed and almost spit it back up all over Eva's head. A little dribble came out the corner of my mouth and down my chin. Kandice was smiling at me. She reached over and wiped my face.

"You're cute," she said.

When we got there in the afternoon Kandice was always fresh out of the shower, her hair dripping down her back and darkening her baseball cap. She always wore a pair of boxers and a men's XL T-shirt, but even in those clothes you could see how good her body was. Her arms and calves were sleekly muscled, not too cut but a real smooth strength there just under the skin, and her tits were beautiful.

She had a ground floor unit with a fenced-in backyard, and we'd put the kids back there and watch them through the screen door. By October, Eva was big enough to sit out there, too, in a bouncy chair, pointing at Tasia and Sirena and Tony and shrieking with joy. When it turned cold, Kandice would make us both coffees with whiskey in them and we'd blow our cigarette smoke out the window above the sink. She paid me in cash, in ones and fives, and it didn't take me that long to figure it out. I mean, I was sheltered but still, the money smelled like perfume and sometimes it was thick with glitter. Kandice said she wasn't ashamed, she just figured it would've been harder to find a babysitter if she'd told the truth up front.

Just before Mom came to pick me up at four, we'd bring the kids in and she'd hand me a bottle of Listerine to cover the alcohol.

THE ELECTRIC BREAST PUMP hurt me but Mom made me use it anyhow. After supper, Cam did the dishes and I pumped so that Mom could have two bottles to take with her into her bedroom. She kept Eva back there while we did homework. And, every Monday, before we started homework, I gave Cam her estrogen and progestogen shots. We did it in our bedroom while Mom was busy with Eva and I stashed the sharps in a

Pedialyte bottle in the back of my closet. It wasn't until much later when Cam and Ben came to visit and Ben called Cam "she" that Mom even paid any attention.

Back in July, when Cam came home from seeing that Charleston doctor, we'd laid across our bed with Eva between us and she told me what the doctor told her. She spread out a pamphlet with words like *androgen blocker, compounded estradiol valerate or cypionate for injection, ventrogluteal muscle, estrogen receptor agonist activity of spironolactone.* Eva grabbed at the corner of the pamphlet, mashing it in her tiny hand. There were pictures of injection sites, one on the butt, one on the hip, one on the arm, one on the leg.

Inside the pamphlet there was another diagram. This one had drawings of tits with measurements and timelines. Over 60 percent growth in the first six months, slowing almost completely after a year. I pictured Cam with perfect little A cups and then my mind had flashed again to Josh McCallister in the back of the school bus, *fucking faggot.* I looked over at Cam and I meant to ask her how she felt but what came out was not a question.

"I'm scared," I said.

She looked at me and her eyes were so tired. "Yeah," she said, "me, too."

The hippies at the health food store might get her pronouns wrong but they probably weren't gonna hurt her, but there were so many other situations I could imagine. I was suddenly terrified. I'd been too distracted, worrying about whether or not she still loved me, worrying about Ben—petty, selfish jealousy. She'd been living with fear every day but it wasn't until that moment that I'd really let it in.

Eva and I started going to the gas station with Cam whenever she needed to fill her van. Mostly it seemed like she could pass as a girl, or maybe most folks noticed her alternative clothes and focused on that, but with me and Eva there they paid less attention to her. I made her promise me she wouldn't stop anywhere between work and home and school, that she wouldn't go to the bathroom in Walmart. She looked at me like I was stupid or slow.

"Why do you think I've always got a piss jar in my car?" she said. "I don't go to public bathrooms anywhere anymore."

Down at the bottom of the pamphlet there was one more reason to worry. When Cam opened Eva's fist and uncurled the paper, I read: "Estrogen carries an elevated risk for blood clotting in the deep veins of the legs or in the lungs and heart." I looked at Cam and pointed to it. Deep vein thrombosis.

"Oh yeah," she said. "I'm s'posed to stop smoking."

After Cam's ventrogluteal shot, we drank Red Bulls and spread our papers out around us in the living room, like real college students, only I was still just doing those homebound packets for my senior year. When I found out I wasn't even gonna get a diploma, just a GED certificate, I quit trying and started just helping Cam with hers instead.

Her English teacher was cute, Cam said. She looked like she would've been friends with us in school, even her teacher outfits were kinda goth. I inspected the teacher's notes on Cam's papers, her tidy handwriting and underlines. She seemed genuinely excited about how good of a student Cam was and I felt the afterglow of her enthusiasm rising off Cam's assignments like a halo and I basked in it, in Cam's potential. I lay back on the couch and read her flashcards for her biology test. The Oxy and Red Bull mixed nice, I was alert and smooth. I listened to Cam's voice stirring over me; each correct answer flowing out of her lips was a stitch toward our future, all starry and bright. I lay there and felt it coming. *Sometimes when I'm going somewhere, I wait. And then somewhere comes to me.*

AT MY SIX-MONTH postpartum checkup, the doctor said it was time to cut off my Oxys. I cried so hard he went for a taper instead. I said I wouldn't be able to work, I wouldn't be able to take care of Eva, I wouldn't be able to even get out of bed. Over time, your body will adjust, he said.

I knew Kandice would help me. And she did, but it wasn't cheap. She quit paying me cash at all and just started giving me Oxy she got from a customer at the club. Even with that, on top of what the doctor was still giving me, it was barely enough.

Kandice said I should start working at the club. I wasn't old enough but all I needed was a professional-grade fake ID and she said I could make back the cost of the ID plus half a dozen Oxy in my first night there.

"New girls always make bank," she said and blew her smoke out of the crack in the window.

"Who'll watch the kids?" I said. They were playing in the slushy snow in the back yard. Through the screen and the dirty window, they were just moving blobs against all that white. I looked at the snow and blinked and I saw the CVS parking lot and my shaky pregnancy test. One year ago.

"Just dance on the weekends, my mom don't work at Tudor's Saturday or Sunday."

I didn't say yes and I didn't say no. I held it, though— the version of me that could work at the club. At first it sounded like a joke, but the longer I held on to it the more it glowed, less like a future and more like a memory, shelved and waiting.

IN DECEMBER CAM told me she was enrolling in the University of Charleston. Double major. English and prelaw. *Law.* I knew Ben was part of her plan before she even said anything about him. I focused my jealousy, gripped it in my teeth. Hating Ben was like sucking on hard candy, I could work it around and around in my mouth endlessly.

I laughed. Cam's eyes flickered. I stared at her face. She hadn't changed a ton with the hormones. She'd never had hardly any facial hair to begin with. If anything, she just looked more than ever like River Phoenix but with a tiny, pretty pair of tits.

"Charleston?" I said.

She nodded. She was stacking dirty plates into the dishwasher. The kitchen and living room were covered in Christmas decorations. Tinsel and plastic Santas on every surface. We'd put them up a few weeks back when Dad was home for a weekend. We'd played Christmas movies on the TV and strung popcorn all together. It had been early for decorations but it was Eva's first Christmas and we were all excited.

"You're gonna drive all the way up there every day for classes?" I said.

"No." Cam closed the dishwasher door.

The woosh and swirl of water spiked my pulse up.

Cam looked at me. "I'm moving in with Ben."

My pulse stopped and then reversed. I looked away. I was always looking away. On the fridge there was a Santa hugging a teddy bear. Eva was sleeping on the blue couch. If I focused closely enough, I could block out everything besides her breath and the swish of the cleaning dishes.

"Shae," Cam said.

I didn't look up.

"Shae, I'm really excited," she said. "My classes sound amazing."

I felt fear like a strike, a physical pain. I pushed my toe into the linoleum. Fear that I was losing her completely. Fear that I'd never find my own way. Fear that I'd never want a future the way that she wanted hers. *Sometimes when I'm going somewhere, I wait. And then somewhere comes to me.* Fear that I'd never stop waiting.

"I'll spend the weekends here with you and Eva," she said.

I rolled my bottom lip in between my teeth. I tried to focus on how much I hated Ben. It was way too scary to admit I might hate Cam so I tried to find a spark in my hatred of Ben, but the truth was I didn't want to feel anything right then. Ten feet away was the coat tree. On the tree was my purse and in the purse was my bottle of Oxy.

When I palmed the bottle open, Cam touched my sleeve and I almost screamed.

"Shae," she said. "How many of those are you taking?"

I let the pill taste coat my tongue.

"I thought they were tapering you off."

"Yeah," I said.

"You're getting 'em from somewhere else."

I put the lid back on the bottle and placed the pills in my purse.

"Shae, they're dangerous," she said. "My mom got hooked on that shit and—"

"I'm in pain," I said.

Cam let out her breath. "I know. But they're real addictive. You gotta be careful."

"I'm in pain," I said again and I focused on it, the strip of pain in my gut and the sound of the dishwasher and the sound of our daughter breathing.

THE FIRST THING Kandice taught me about private dances was *slow down*. All they get is one song unless they pay you again. An average song is two and a half minutes, you don't have to wear yourself out. If you chat for the first thirty seconds, you're down to two minutes.

"Whatever you do, don't try that stupid upside-down backward, ass-in-their-face move," Kandice told me.

She had me pinned when she said this. We were on the couch in her bedroom. She'd put a movie on for the kids and now she was training me, one foot against my hip, one hand gripping.

They all think they want cuddly lambs, she said, but really they want you in control and the whole thing is easier if you've got them pinned: left foot at the joint of his hip, your heel positioned so that it digs into the couch cushion but if he makes the wrong move it slips into his crotch, and your right hand intertwined with his left, like you're holding hands only you're actually holding his whole arm down and keeping it from moving. In this position he'll feel like you're all up on him, your left leg is touching him and you're holding his hand, but really he's far away from all your best bits.

"Slow down and isolate," she said. "They love that shit. Make them look at your pussy and then bring their eyes up slowly."

She was wearing her boxers and T-shirt but I could see her tits moving. When I watched them, I felt a heat spread out between my legs and my throat froze. I couldn't swallow my own spit so I looked away. There was a Willie Nelson poster tacked to Kandice's wall and the late evening shadows spread all blue across her bed.

"You try," she said. "With the shoes."

The shoes were six-inch candy-apple-red peep-toes. I was so unsteady Kandice couldn't quit laughing.

"You're s'posed to jiggle not stumble," she said.

I was wearing my bra and panties, my C scar visible through the lace. I was so nervous I was sweating despite the cold. The heat in Kandice's apartment only half worked but my armpits and hands were slick. Cam was the only person who'd ever seen my body before and that was prepregnancy and even then I'd tried to hide it as best I could.

I lifted my left leg and almost collapsed but grabbed the couch instead.

"Anytime you gotta grab, anytime you almost fall, make it like it was planned," Kandice said. "Like you wanted to touch them."

Cat Power's "I've Been Thinking" was playing from Kandice's phone and behind it I could hear Winnie the Pooh.

I grabbed Kandice's hand and leaned in toward her.

"Good," she said and then she reached between my legs for a pack of cigarettes. "Hold on, let me get this lit. A lot of them smoke, you gotta navigate the cigarettes without getting burnt."

I rolled my shoulders so that my tits jiggled. And then I didn't know what else to do so I did it again.

"Wait, watch," Kandice said and then she flipped me, just like that, I was on the bottom again and she was the one dancing over me, cigarette between her lips. Her eyes were deep and wet. "Just watch, okay."

"Be my boy," Cat Power crooned, "Be my boy, be my boy, be my boyyyyy."

Kandice's cigarette was in her left hand now and her lips were on my neck, the end of her nose cold against my skin. I was shaking worse than I had been before. I could taste her kiss already, how smoky and warm her tongue would be. She leaned back, took a drag on her cigarette and traced my clavicle with her fingernail and then she moved in quick.

"Don't worry," she breathed into my ear. "I'm not gonna fuck you."

"WEEKENDS?" MOM SAID. "Why is a telecommunication center even open on the weekends?" She was standing at the sink with a bottle brush in her hand.

"It's not the weekend everywhere," I said. "Time difference."

Her hands dripped soapy water onto the rug.

"Kandice will give me a ride," I said and I saw us then, in our beige cubicles, calling all the far-off corners of the world. But the image got mixed with reality and I saw Kandice making phone calls in only a G-string. I almost giggled. I liked that there was a version of me that Mom knew nothing about.

"But weekends." Mom shook her head. "That's the only time Cam's gonna be here."

"Yeah," I said. "So? They pay twice as much for weekend night shifts."

The house was full up with already gone energy. Like when you're parked beside the tracks and the train starts to move and suddenly you're rolling but the train is the only one passing through. I had to grab some sort of momentum.

CAM MUST'VE MENTIONED her worries about the Oxy cause Mom started asking questions she'd never asked before. I don't think she would've said anything without Cam mentioning it. I used my new job as proof—if I were having trouble with the pills, I wouldn't be going out and getting a new job, now would I?

I quit taking them in front of her or Cam. I cleaned all the pill bottles out of my room. But Mom still worried. I heard her on the phone with her sister when she thought I was sleeping.

"I should've taken her to church," she said. "Something to fall back on in times like this." Her voice stretched. "But you remember the blood? How it come all down her face." Mom's voice stopped and I gripped the blankets. "Preacher Wilson's wife. Said he'd been hitting her for years." Mom sounded like she was pleading. "I swore, once I was old enough, I'd never go back to church."

ON CAM'S FINAL week at Eden's, she worked overtime doing inventory. Her last day, she called me in the afternoon, asked if I wanted to come by later, bring Chinese food for her and the other girl and help finish up so she didn't have to stay so late. I got Mom to drop me at five fifteen. I came in through the back alley. I told Mom that Cam would give me a ride home. Cam had never asked me to help out at work before. I let my rage about her upcoming move to Charleston fall to my ankles and grow cold.

In the alley there were piles of sloppy early snow fading in the warm breath of the laundromat vents. A group of crows picked through wet garbage, testing cigarette butts. My hands were full of hot Styrofoam and up ahead the clouds were breaking. I turned the knob without spilling the food and stepped into the back hall. The lights upstairs were all off but Cam's voice was there. Right away it reached me. Her voice and then the other girl's.

"I don't know."

"But you said she's been taking more lately."

In the darkened sills of the front windows, tiny jeweled globes, golden holders, bits of mirror.

"I know, but it's not about Shae."

From behind me, through the broken clouds, the sun was reaching desperately.

"I just can't live here anymore. I'm not me when I'm here."

The sun hit the shop door and I harnessed it. I harnessed every bit of that moment, Cam's voice, the rays, the dust motes floating, I turned them all into my name, like turning some great wheel. I had the power to do that then, grab the spokes and turn everything to be about me. I can't do it anymore, warp things into such a beautiful peacocking pity, but then, oh, then! Even the last rays of sun were about me in that place at that exact moment. I'd used the back door for no reason but if I'd come in the front, there was a jangle of bells that would've silenced everyone. Here I was though, rooted. I felt the power of my own pity rise, shimmering. I meant nothing. This was so much worse than thinking that Cam was leaving me because of the drugs, because of the catheter, because, because. I meant nothing. I'd always suspected and now I had proof! I gripped it and I held on. I would ride it like a comet through all the next months of my life. I could bury it for a while and then pull it back up. It was glorious. It was crucial. It made all my fuckups make sense. I was always in the hallways of life, always outside listening in at just the right wrong moment. And later, in that drop-down time whenever I started to feel guilty or scared of what I was doing, I'd pull that beautiful pity up and brandish it, paint it in stripes across myself. I rode it out of the store and down the alley, hot Styrofoam abandoned and the crows feasting.

6 | SOUTHERN X-POSURE

The first dancer I met, after Kandice, was Raven. Kandice convinced her to let me come in early and practice on the pole. The parking lot was empty except for one car when we got there at five, little bits of snow blowing sideways across the cement and the sun gone behind the trees already. Kandice had told me to buy Raven a Subway steak sandwich and I had it sitting, still hot, on my lap.

"Well, come on," Kandice said.

With the neon lights turned off, the building looked like a bunker. I could hear the highway behind me as we walked.

Kandice knocked on the back door, and when no one

answered she pulled out her cellphone. "Yeah, we're around back here," she said and put the phone away and lit a cigarette.

I was carrying the Subway bag delicate in my hands in front of me, and in my backpack I had a hand-me-down lime green teddy from Kandice and a pair of white knee-high pleather boots. Boots were easier to start in, Kandice said, not as sexy maybe but also less likely to kill you.

The door opened. Raven was tall and very pale, with wrinkles around her eyes and mouth and dyed black hair. "Don't let the cold in, it's already freezing as hell in here," she said through a cigarette clenched between her teeth.

"Hell ain't freezing," Kandice said.

"What the fuck ever." Raven locked the door behind us and walked away.

The dressing room was long and narrow with mirrors all along the left wall and chairs pulled up to a counter spilling over with cans of hairspray, bags of baby wipes, curling irons, straighteners, brushes, and lip gloss. Raven sat in an easy chair at the far end of the room with a spill of silver sequined fabric across her lap and a needle in her hand. The TV beside her was playing *The Office*. Michael Scott was accidentally wearing women's pants.

Raven looked up. "Welcome to the fucking pigsty," she said. "I keep threatening the girls if they don't get this shit cleaned up, I'm gonna sweep it all into the trash one night."

I nodded. "I brought you a steak sub," I said. "Extra mayo."

"Lay it there." Raven nodded toward the TV. "So, Kandi says you're still nursing?"

I set the sub on top of the television and stepped back.

"Uh, yeah," I said.

Raven exhaled. "Alright, you're gonna have to wear pasties. You'll need to pump right before you start and probably again midway through the night and put on pasties. Even so, you'll drip, but hell, some men like it."

As she talked, I could feel my nipples perk and express, my sports bra growing damp.

"You wanna see the pole?" Kandice said.

I nodded and walked back toward her.

"Oh and hey," Raven said through a bite of sandwich. "Pick a name that's not too different from your real one, otherwise you're liable to forget who you are and not notice when they call you up on stage."

Kandice held the curtain aside for me. "Raven still dances some," she said. "Well, whenever she wants to, I guess, but she's in charge of the schedule and everything else, too. She's been doing this forever. She worked at the Pink Pony up in Cross Lanes when Jack Whittaker went there."

"Who?" I said. It was so dark in the main room I was afraid to move forward.

Kandice walked around me and turned on an overhead fluorescent light, thin and yellow-green. It made the room look like a terrarium. "Jack Whittaker. Powerball winner."

"Oh," I said.

"Come on, really? You didn't hear about that? He left his Suburban running out front of the Pink Pony with five hundred thousand dollars in the passenger seat and somebody snatched it."

"Oh, shit," I said.

Kandice laughed. "Oh, shit is right. Don't ask Raven about it unless you wanna hear about two hours of who it was that really killed Brandi Bragg."

"Who's Brandi Bragg?"

Kandice looked at me like I was crazy. "When were you born again?"

I opened my mouth to answer before I realized it might be a trick question. I suddenly couldn't remember the date of birth on my fake ID.

"Alright, get up here," Kandice said, climbing onto the stage.

I set my bag down at one of the tables and boosted myself up.

"Honestly, you're wasting your time learning anything more than this." Kandice walked to the pole, grabbed it, leaned back and let the crook of her knee catch. She spun backward down until her knees hit the stage. "The kinda guys that come in here, they don't want Cirque du Soleil. They want tits and pussy and ass."

I walked over toward the pole.

"Take off your pants," Kandice said.

I froze.

"Your skin grips better than your clothes."

Kandice went into the dressing room and left me alone with the mirror. I could see the far end of the room reflected back, the red pleather stools and the liquor bottles lined up all glittery. You'd think time had stopped and pocketed us. An Old Milwaukee sign blinked. I'd never been inside a bar. There I was, though, or a slightly warped reflection of me at least, pink cotton panties, striped socks and a Mountaineers sweatshirt. It lodged in my brain but wouldn't quite make sense, the fact that I could just walk in and act like this was me. Cam was the first thing in my life that wasn't arranged by someone else. I'd reached out for her and everything since then came from that, but the lines weren't straight. Maybe that's what you called Real Life. It didn't feel wrong and it didn't feel right, either way it was here in front of me.

I practiced spinning for a better part of an hour, my skin all gooseflesh, palms sweating. If I avoided the reflection of my ass, I didn't feel too embarrassed. After a while Kandice poked her head out.

"Okay, little mama," she said, "what's your new name?"

I picked Shane but Kandice heard Shine and that stuck.

Around six thirty the front-house manager, Mickie, and the bouncer, Allen, arrived. I pulled my jeans on quick as the other girls started dribbling in through the front door, carrying duffels on their shoulders and paper takeout food bags. Raven called me into the back.

"Hey ladies," Raven said over the chit-chat and rustle of burger wrappers. Everyone looked up at the mirror. Raven and I were reflected there, her black hair shimmery across her shoulders and me, baby-fat bloated with my backpack on and my sneakers held stupidly in my left hand.

"I want you all to welcome our newest girl," Raven said. "This is Shine. She's starting tonight."

I looked at Raven in the mirror and my eyes blew up big. I'd thought I was just coming in to practice.

"What's your song?" she asked.

"Song?"

"Every girl's got a song."

"Oh."

"Like your signature. The DJ'll have it cued for all your stage sets."

"Oh."

Raven raised her eyebrows in the mirror.

"Uh. 'Dark Horse,'" I said.

"'Dark Horse'?"

"Katy Perry."

Raven turned and looked down the room. "Don't Tara dance to that one?"

"Uh-uh, not really anymore," a blond girl said. "I think she likes that Paula Abdul song now. Something about a snake."

"Alright, but if Tara claims 'Dark Horse,' what's your backup?"

I looked at the floor, scattered with bobby pins. "'Toxicity,'" I said. "System of a Down."

"Well that's different." Raven laughed.

Kandice made a space for me beside her at the counter. The

only available chair was a metal folding one that was so cold on my skin it made my teeth ache.

"Don't worry too much about your hair and makeup," Kandice said. "I mean, do whatever you want, but what the guys notice is perfume, lipstick, tits, pussy, and ass."

"Hey, don't be so ugly about it," the girl beside Kandice said. She had dyed red hair that she was curling, lock by lock, into long Shirley Temple spirals. "Just cuz you don't give a fuck what you look like don't mean she has to."

Kandice snorted. "It's a waste of time and money."

The girl leaned around behind Kandice. She was holding her curling iron in place with one hand and reaching out to me with the other. "Hey, sweetie, I'm Glory," she said.

Kandice took her baseball cap off, pulled her hair straight back from her face, and tied it into a half-up, half-down situation. She put on a thick coat of deep red twenty-four-hour-superstay lipstick, a lace-frilled pink pushup bra that turned her tits into a jiggling shelf, and a white G-string that I would later see glowed under the black lights. She buckled her six-inch candy-apple-red peep toe heels and she was done. She got up and moved her chair over to face the television set.

"Hey, hey," Glory said when she saw me watching. "Just cuz men are stupid don't mean we don't need to have self-respect. I like doing my hair and face."

When I said nothing, she went on. "If you ever need tips on doing your eyes, River is the best. She sits down there." Glory pointed to a tattooed woman at the far end of the counter. "I'll ask her for you if you want."

I forced a quick smile. "Thanks, I'm okay, thanks," I said. I liked the way that everything in that room wove around me without demanding much.

When I took the hand-me-down teddy out of my backpack, Glory glanced at it and said, "Ooh, honey, I don't know if that green is really your color."

"It don't matter what she wears," Kandice snapped without even turning around. "She's fresh meat."

It was two days before Christmas and business was slow. All the men had already spent all their money on gifts. By eight o'clock there were still no customers. We huddled in the back and watched *The Office*. The episode with the Dundies came on and Pam got drunk and kissed Jim and then Pam was drunk in the parking lot and she kept saying, "Hey, Jim, hey, can I ask you a question?"

There were fifteen of us around that TV, silent, tensed and breathless, though I'd guess we'd all seen it before.

"Yeah, of course," Jim said.

"Okay," Pam said and giggled. "Thank you."

"That's not really a question," Jim said.

And then Pam got into Angela's car and drove away and Jim looked at the camera and our stomachs all did a big old loop and dip. I felt the tension in my fingertips, my hands jammed into fists. *That's not really a question*, Jim's voice said in a loop in my head. There were so many questions I should've asked Cam, so many questions I probably should've asked myself.

"Girrrls!" Mickie called through the stage door. "Where the hell are you?"

"There's no guys out there," Raven said.

"So?" Mickie looked around the room and his eyes settled on me. "Who's that?"

"Shine," Raven said.

"Why's she got that shit on her titties?"

I felt my nipples stiffen, felt the glue I'd used to fix the pasties in place. I felt all my skin, the pudge around my waist and my C-scar and my thighs where they met. The lace teddy was itchy. I could smell my own sweat.

"So she don't squirt milk in your face," Raven said.

"Oh." Mickie nodded. He had a dyed blond ponytail but he hadn't gotten around to making his mustache match yet. "I want everybody out on the floor now."

We shuffled out and crowded around the bar and Mickie poured everybody eggnog out of a big Kroger brand carton.

"Alright listen up," he said but before he could finish his eyes got stuck on Glory's crotch. "That's real nice," he said, pointing to her bellybutton ring: a mistletoe sprig that dangled on a little chain to just above her pubic hair line. "Okay, alright, it's always slow this time of year but you know it's not cuz the guys don't love you. We just gotta remind them that we're here. I had an idea and I got Allen working on part of it, but I want you girls to finish up your nog and get to work on your end."

His idea was that we would all climb up on the roof of the club with a blow-up Santa and line up like we were reindeer and then Allen would spotlight us from the parking lot. Folks would be able to see us all the way from the highway.

"Raven, I want you to run up to the Walmart for a Santa," Mickie said. "The rest of you figure out your outfits or whatever. Maybe you shouldn't wear such high heels on the roof?"

I looked over at Kandice. She rolled her eyes, downed the rest of her eggnog, and put her fingers up to her temples like the barrel of a gun. *Boom.* I smiled.

The girls were all screaming. "Have you lost your fucking mind? I don't make enough money to ever!" "Where in the fuck did you!" "Fuck off!" "Yeah right." And Mickie kept repeating "Trust me, trust me, there's a reason I'm the manager here, trust me."

Allen came out of a back room with a snarled nest of extension cords in his arms. He was sweating and grunting.

Mickie pulled out a wad of cash. "Raven, get some Santa hats for the girls, too. Whatever else is cute."

Raven was shaking her head but she took the cash and tucked it in her back pocket.

"Strings of lights as the reins!" Mickie said, grinning. "You know, the reindeer reins, like to string you all together."

The front door crashed open and we all turned.

There was a burly guy with a Heartland hat standing there. Behind him, through the open door, snow was blowing all up and down and sideways, a smudged trail of highway lights just barely visible through it.

"Fuck this night," the trucker said.

He told us the blizzard had started about forty-five minutes ago, down around Wytheville, and then when he got up just before the Princeton exit another sixteen-wheeler had jackknifed in the middle of the road.

I flinched. Every time I heard "jackknifed" I pictured Daddy, his body thrown through the windshield of his rig. When I got done picturing that, the trucker was playing with Glory's bellybutton ring and I felt another panic coming. What if Daddy were to come in here? I'd never ever thought of him as one to go to a titty bar but Southern X-Posure was literally right off of I-77 and I knew he drove this route all the time.

"You okay?" Kandice said.

I nodded and then grabbed her arm and pulled her away from the bar. "My daddy's a trucker," I said. "And I just got to thinking—"

She cut me off before I could even finish. "It happens," she said. "Cindy's daddy come in when she first started working and both she and him was shocked as all hell but he made this big fuss about this being his bar and she should quit and whatever. Mickie and Raven decided Cindy won't work Tuesdays and Thursdays and then Rusty can come in. He's not allowed any other days."

I wasn't sure that story made me feel any better but Mickie was shouting and I let it distract me.

"No, it's even more of a reason to do it," he was saying. "All that traffic stopped on the road and they've got nothing to look at but us."

"No way, it's a fucking blizzard out there. My girls are not going out there," Raven said.

But Mickie kept at it, until the trucker pointed out there was a lot of cops on the highway and then Allen said what if they blamed us, like as a distraction that caused the wreck. Mickie gave it up after that but he kept repeating every so often, *That was a good idea, that was a real good idea.*

The trucker got a private dance from Glory in the champagne room while the rest of us drank eggnog. After a while Colton came in. I didn't know him yet of course, but even then, before I heard his whole story, I could see the bruised puppy-dog look in his eyes. He was wearing Carhartts and an oversized sweatshirt and when he slouched up to the bar, Kandice walked over to him. They talked for a while and then I looked up and saw Kandice waving at me.

"Hey, this is Colton," she said. "Colton, this is Shae."

Later Kandice told me that Colton was who she'd been getting my Oxy from. Colton didn't buy private dances from the girls and he didn't even sit at the stage, but he would buy us drinks and cigarettes. He just liked to get high and shoot the shit with somebody and he didn't want to be at home so he'd come up to the club, nurse a couple beers, and buy us girls whatever we wanted. Kandice didn't treat him like a customer but more like another employee. I guess that was why she told him my real name.

It didn't take me and Colton more than half an hour to figure out our connections. He was married to the older sister of Chrissie Hughes who went to school with me. Chrissie Hughes, in the back of the bus, who wouldn't sneeze to mess up her makeup. Colton was married to her sister Mistie. He had worked for their dad at the quarry until he got a job on a fracking pipeline up in Pennsylvania. He'd go up to the frack fields and work a couple weeks and then come home for a little bit. One day he was working with a guy, locking the pipes into place. One of them had to hold it while the other slugged it with a sledgehammer. The guy missed and hit Colton's hand. Broke almost every bone. The doctor put him on Oxy.

Whenever he got to this point in the story, Colton would lift his bandaged right hand and wink. "Won the lottery," he'd say.

Eventually the doctor had stopped his prescription. That's when he'd sawed the cast off, rebroke his own hand, and went to a different doctor. By the time I met him, he'd done it three times.

Colton was a funny one. He wasn't handsome exactly but you could get to thinking that he was or that he would've been if life hadn't used him as a punching bag. but then you'd be around him a while and you'd realize that he wasn't anybody to feel sorry for. He'd always been on top. He'd played football, he'd got the prom queen girl, he'd got a super-good-paying job and now he'd got a steady supply of drugs. Won the lottery.

That same winter I met him, Colton found a baby weasel or something in the ditch beside the parking lot one night. He'd seen it moving in his headlights. He brought it inside the club. It was tiny, with dark, shiny fur and a long tail that it tucked up over its nose. He was freaking out about it, wanting some-body to look on their phone and find out what to feed it. It was another slow night and we all crowded around. Somebody found a shoebox and made a little bed. Somebody else, Kandice maybe, tried to feed it a Little Debbie oatmeal cream pie. But the animal, whatever it was, died. And Colton cried. I didn't even see him cry when I watched him break his own fingers a few months later, but that night he cried. When Mickie saw it he started screaming about rabies. *Get that shit out*, he said and so Colton put it back into the sequin nest inside the shoebox and carried it out by the dumpster and lit it on fire.

BUT THAT'S JUMPING ahead. On that night, my first night, just before Christmas, all Colton and I did was talk about Chrissie and Mistie Hughes. Or he talked and I listened. All I said was that I knew Chrissie, which wasn't even true. I knew of Chrissie. Still, I was impressed that this me could sit up at a bar and say anything.

After a while a group of guys came in. Colton never acted jealous and never tried to keep any of us there at the bar with him if there were other customers. That's another thing that made him feel more like an unofficial employee. "Go on," he'd say, "gotta make that money, girl, or steal it somehow."

The guys that came in were construction worker buddies trying to throw a party for their friend who was getting a divorce. There were six of them. The divorced man was like a black hole among them. You looked at him too long and you started to feel every good thought or feeling that was ever in you sucked out and blown away.

We got the stage rotation up and going for them. Each girl got two songs. Glory turned herself upside down at the top of the pole and then lowered herself bit by bit while "Cherry Pie" screamed from the speakers. All I could do was spin twice on the crook of my knee and then crawl over to the edge of the stage where the men lined up. Their ringleader was something of a regular at the club and he noticed right away that I was new. He kept saying, "I like you. I like you." And then after a while he decided his friend needed a private dance.

The champagne room was a pleather couch in the corner past the stage, sectioned off with plastic latticework and semi-opaque curtains. The men outside the "room" could see that there was something going on in there but they couldn't quite see what.

I led the sad man in by his hand. "Merry almost Christmas," I said and then I positioned myself like Kandice had taught me to do, one foot on his thigh, one hand twined with his fingers. He looked down at my foot in his lap and then up past my tits to my face. His eyes were glazed with so much more than just alcohol.

"It stays in the stairway," he said. "Her voice and the anger, too. I paid them to clean it."

My breath caught in my throat. I looked away from him.

"It's in the oven and on the windowsills."

I wiggled my hips but he wasn't watching.

"How am I ever gonna turn around and not love her?" he said, and his voice was so desperate I wanted to punch it away.

From the main floor we heard whoops and hollers. "Well, Bill, how is she?" a voiced called. This seemed to break the sad man out of his dream.

"Frank's a good guy," he said to me. "He can't fix it and he knows it and so he wants to spend money on me."

I nodded. I took my foot off his thigh.

"You can just dance a little or whatever and at least that way you make some money," he said.

I nodded again. "It's my first night," I said. "I don't really know what I'm doing."

The sad man smiled. "It goes like this," he said and he moved his left hand in a circle and then his right. I mirrored him. We moved like mimes.

"All they can see from out there is movement," he said. "We'll just keep moving."

We moved our hands in big circles silently and when my right tit started leaking milk, we both laughed.

When we got back to the main floor the sad man had counted the songs for me. Five of them. He told Frank he owed me two hundred dollars. "And don't be stingy, man, tip her well. It's almost Christmas."

In the dressing room, Kandice told me to put my clothes on. It was time to drive back to Render, the snow was getting real bad. Raven said we could stay at her place but Kandice wanted to get home. Tomorrow was Christmas Eve.

It took us twice as long as it should've to get back. We smoked all of Kandice's cigarettes. The headlights formed a weak cone and we were barreling right straight through the guts and the heart of everything, right straight into the terrible night. And all I could hear was the sad man's words over and over again. *It stays in the stairway*, he said. *How am I ever gonna turn around and not love her?* His hands moved in big slow circles in the headlights. *We'll just keep moving.*

Kandice's apartment was barely warm and we bundled right into her bed. I took my layers off under the covers. I still had the pasties glued on. Kandice got up and got me a warm rag to soak the glue off.

"Tomorrow, you're gonna want to take a long bath," she said. "With lots of Epsom salts. Crawling on the stage on your knees like that, it takes a while to get your body used to it."

Through the window, in the yellow streetlight, the snow-flakes swirled and lifted. I pulled her to me, my mouth on her neck and then her lips. We kissed for a while and then she pulled away.

"Baby girl," she said. "I'm not gonna fuck you."

"Why not?" I said. When I talked my breath was visible over the bed.

"You're underage," she said.

"So?"

"It's illegal."

"So?"

"You'll have it to use against me," she said. Her hand was warm on my belly, her chin resting against my neck. I could feel her jaw moving when she spoke.

"I would never," I said.

She raised up on one elbow, brushed my hair away from my face, and kissed my cheek. "That's the thing," she said. "You think you'd never until you do."

She fell asleep and I lay in the dark and listened to the snowflakes hit the window screen and thought about what kind of scumbag would do that, turn on a friend like that. I didn't see it then but of course already there was a shadow of me in that same room, ten months from then, picking my way past dirty laundry to her back-of-the-closet cash spot. Already there was the shadow of me turning to Colton in the doorway and saying, "I know her schedule at the club, she won't be home for hours yet."

7 | HONEY FAKER

We never would've caught Jonas's mom's fiancé if we'd been one aisle over or a few minutes late. But that's jumping ahead. We didn't start out in Costco that day. It was Eva's first birthday. Mom drove me and Eva up to Charleston. We were supposed to have supper together, Cam and Ben and me and Mom and Eva.

Cam met us outside Ben's condo on the sidewalk. I didn't know yet that I wasn't allowed inside. I thought Cam just happened to be out there when we arrived. It was a really warm May day and she was wearing a NIN T-shirt with the sleeves cut off. Ben was up in DC for work, driving back that day, and he was gonna meet us at Shoney's but we had hours left before that. Eva was so little we didn't know how to celebrate her. She couldn't really tell one day from the next. Mom had errands to run so we all tagged along. Beside the Jo-Ann Fabrics store, there was a nail salon.

"Let's all go get our nails done!" I said. I was cash happy at that point. I was working at the club every weekend and I still had my Oxy script plus money to buy more pills from Colton to supplement with. I was high and happy and flush with cash.

"Come on," I said. "My treat!"

The girls in the salon loved Eva. They passed her around between them as they did our nails. Oxblood for Cam, electric pink on me, and French tips for Mom. I asked them to set rhinestones into my gel.

"Really?" Cam said.

"You want some?" I was feeling so happy to be with her. To be with her and Mom and Eva. I wanted Ben to never show up at Shoney's. For this day to never end.

Cam shook her head. "You got somebody you're trying to impress at that telecommunication center?"

I wrinkled my nose and laughed. I pictured the work me that Mom and Cam thought of—headset, Muzak, list of numbers for dialing. It sort of hurt that they assumed I'd be fine with a job that boring.

"How's work going?" Cam said.

I hated it when she talked to me like that, all older and distant. She'd been leaving me messages—texts, and then when

I didn't text back, voicemail messages—asking straight up about the Oxy, about tapering off. Did I need help, she said. I quit listening, let the messages build up unheard, little red notifications like tiny jewels at the bottom of my phone.

"Work's fine," I said. "If you don't want rhinestones you should at least get them to put a design on your nails. Come on."

Eva was giggling hysterically while one of the girls tickled her belly.

"I don't think the chemicals in here are probably good for her to breathe. Her little lungs," Cam said. "We should go."

We had lunch downtown at some taco place Cam chose. It was okay, overpriced. I asked Mom to order us beers and Cam and Mom looked at me weird.

"Come on," I said. "It's Eva's birthday. Let's celebrate!"

I knew I was treating it like it was *my* birthday but I didn't care.

We walked down by the river after lunch. Mom asked what time we were meeting Ben, and Cam said she hadn't heard back from him yet, didn't know when he was gonna get on the road. I noticed then that she'd been checking her phone over and over again.

"He hasn't texted me," she said. "I'm gonna call him."

The sun was pouring over everything, making me happy, drowsy. There were buttercups growing thick on the bank and the river was smooth that day. Downstream where the rich people's houses sprouted into four, five stories, I could see their boats bobbing.

"It's a perfect boat day," I said. "We should be on a boat today!"

Mom looked at me with a tight, funny smile. I glanced back at Cam. She'd dropped behind, mumbling something into her phone.

"He's probably still in meetings," she called to us. "I left him a message to let us know."

"Let Eva see the flowers," I said to Mom, who was holding her on her hip. "Come on, it's her birthday!"

We all sat down on the bank, and Eva crawled, her head a golden puff among the golden flowers. I watched her inspect a blade of grass with her tiny, delicate fingers and my heart felt so swollen it made me sick. I wanted everyone to recognize the whopping perfection of this moment but Cam was checking her phone again.

"Let's stay here forever," I said.

Cam laughed. "We should be careful Eva doesn't get sunburnt."

Eva crawled toward a flowering cherry. Mom followed her.

"I need to rest for a minute," I said. I was lying back in the grass, staring at Cam: her hair laying softly over one shoulder, the precise line of her neck where it swept up to her skull. I still knew what her skin tasted like but I hadn't touched it in six months.

"What do you think you're gonna do?" she said. She was looking out at the river.

"What do you mean?"

"Do you wanna go to college?" she asked without turning her head. "You just need to get your GED first, right?"

I made a sound like a strangle-laugh. I wanted to say *if you hadn't gotten me pregnant, I'd be graduating high school right now*, but my tongue was too thick and wouldn't cooperate. And even though it was technically true, that wasn't our story. Accidental teenage pregnancy, life plans derailed—that was soap-opera material. Our story was better than that. I watched the cords move in Cam's neck, watched so closely I could feel them beneath my fingers. It occurred to me that she knew nothing of me now. Working at Southern X-Posure was the first time I'd actually ever done anything on my own. Making friends with Cam had split me from Mom for a moment but soon she'd been incorporated into our family. This was the first time I'd done anything entirely on my own. Cam thought I did nothing. She checked her phone.

"I don't work at a telecommunications center," I said.

Cam looked at me then.

I glanced to make sure that Mom was still out of earshot.

"I work at a strip club," I said.

Cam put her phone away. I smiled. It was so stupid, but I thought if she knew that people paid money to see my body, I thought if I could surprise her, she would see me again.

"Really?"

I nodded. "I work there with my girlfriend, Kandice," I lied. Kandice was certainly not my girlfriend but it sounded better that way.

"Really?" Cam said again. "You're dating that fuckup you used to babysit for and working with her at a titty bar? That's your plan?"

I couldn't find anything familiar in her eyes. I knew right away that I'd messed up but I shrugged and tried to brush it off. Later, when the lawyer used the club against me to take away custody, I would try to pretend like it wasn't Cam, like it was all Ben's idea, but the truth is, someone had to tell Ben in the first place. Back then, I was so full up thinking about Ben hurting me, I didn't think about me hurting Cam and Eva. Cam had tried to tell me about her mom but I didn't really listen. I didn't stop and think about the shadows of her life in mine. I don't know Cam's mom's name and I don't know if I ever did. I wanna call her Arlette, Arlene, Eileen. A dancing queen. Snakeskin. Rhinestone jeans. Back then, it never crossed my mind that Cam was worrying about Eva ending up with a childhood like hers.

Mom called out to us from down the riverbank and I got up, wiped my pants off, and tried to forget Cam's look. I knew that Mom had been itching to use Cam's Costco card ever since Cam mentioned, months before, that she and Ben had a membership. Mom hadn't said anything to Cam because she didn't want to seem greedy. But I knew she wanted it and I wanted to use Cam, so I said we should go.

"We've got time to kill," I said. "I mean, Ben hasn't called you back, right?"

Cam glanced at her phone, shook her head.

I nursed Eva in the car and she got sleepy but she woke right up as soon as we got inside Costco. Eva loved riding in buggies. I jumped up on the other end. "Come on, push us!" I said.

Except for the fact that I fed her from my tits, Eva and I could've been sisters. Cam and Mom, the parents. Cam had only ever been a year older than me but somehow over the past six months she'd leapt far ahead, deep into adulthood, while I remained—no, I'd circled back.

Mom wasn't with us when we saw him. We'd left her in the baking aisle and were headed I don't know where when Cam stopped the buggy. I looked at her and then looked where she was looking. There was a man in a red beret hefting gallon jugs of generic honey-corn syrup blend off the shelf. Beside him was a hippie chick, her bra-less nipples on full display through her peasant blouse. I looked back at Cam. She was frozen, watching him grab jug after jug of honey.

"Who is that?" I said.

Cam didn't take her eyes off him. "Jonas's mom's fiancé."

And I remembered him then. He'd sold honey at Eden's store when Cam worked there and he used to come in all the time to check on his sales. He was cocky, always talking about his apiary in Raleigh County, how he had such a connection to the bees he didn't even need to wear a protective suit. Bee charmer. Cam always laughed after he left, said he'd watched *Fried Green Tomatoes* one too many times. Problem was he didn't have even half the charm of Idgie. Jonas told us that his mom had begged to see the bees, to watch him working, but he never let her. She wanted to have the wedding there.

The hippie chick reached up and kissed him, brushed a strand of hair under his beret. She was way too young to be Jonas's mom.

"Hey, what are you doing?" Cam said.

I was shocked to see her walking toward him. It was the girl that bothered Cam more than the honey, I think.

Beret's face flashed from confusion to recognition to terror.

"Oh, hey, Cam . . . uh, Cameron . . . Cam, right?"

Cam looked back and forth between him and the girl.

"Hey," Beret said. His hands were fidgeting with the handle of a jug of honey. He looked down and let go real quick.

"Hey, I know how this must look, right." He attempted a laugh and stared past Cam toward me and Eva. "That's your kid, huh? Cute kid."

The girl looked annoyed. "Who is this?" she said, and when Beret said nothing, she turned to Cam. "Who are you?"

"Why?" Cam said. She was standing firm in the middle of the aisle, ignoring the girl.

Eva was burbling. I picked her up out of the buggy just to have something to do.

"Look, this was just gonna be a temporary thing until I can get the hives going again." Beret looked down at his Birkenstocks and then back up. "Please don't tell anyone. Please don't tell Shelly, don't tell Jonas, please."

I bounced Eva. His face was disgusting and fascinating to watch.

A lot of people would've liked having the power Cam had. Beret was right there in her hands. She did not like it. The more Beret begged the sadder Cam looked. I know she wished she'd never seen him, never known about this mess. She did not promise not to tell but she did help him put all the honey back.

NEITHER OF US mentioned it to Mom when we found her in the freezer aisle, but it sat there among us, ruining the mood.

Cam looked at her phone three times in the check-out and again when we got outside.

"Go on," Cam said to Mom and me. "I have to call Ben. I don't know what's going on with him."

When she got to the car her face was crumpled. "No answer." She shrugged.

"I bet he forgot to charge his phone," Mom said. "Or else he's in a place with no service."

"In DC?" I said from the back seat where I was nursing Eva. "It's not like he's on the top of a mountain."

"Hey, now," Mom said, frowning at me. "There's gonna be a simple reason and we'll find it out soon. There always is. That's the way it goes when Rodney doesn't call me and I get in a tizzy. It's always for nothing."

Mom couldn't help herself. I knew she wanted me and Cam to be together and Ben was in the way of that but Mom loved Cam. She didn't like to see her worry. And she didn't like to ask questions. She never said anything about Cam and Ben and she never said a thing about Cam's transition, until we got into the custody battle at least. Mostly I think she was a lot like me, or I was like her. She didn't like change so she didn't question anything.

BEN DIDN'T CALL until we were halfway through our meal at Shoney's. Mom was feeding Eva mashed potatoes and Eva was spitting them back out. She wasn't very good at eating anything besides my milk.

"Hey, hello?" Cam said into her phone. "Where the fuck are you?"

She slid out of the booth and walked toward the front doors and I lost her voice, but once she was outside in the parking lot, I could see her through the windows. She was talking a lot and waving her hands around, her oxblood nails. I couldn't hear any of her words but she looked angry and it was making my heart skip and jump, my lips twitch into an almost smile. She was walking in circles, down the sidewalk, through the flowerbed, across the handicapped spot and back. The wind was blowing her hair into her face and she kept tucking it behind her ear, her piercings glinting in the evening sun.

"I never knew you two to fight. Seems like you always got along great," Mom said to me.

I looked at her. She was drinking her Diet Coke, her lipstick smudging the straw. Her words had shattered my tiny almost-hope. And now I just sat there with my mouth slightly open, looking past her, out the window at Cam. Mom had never asked about our breakup and I had never said a word because there was no breakup. She was right, we'd never fought. But we also maybe never dated? I was too afraid of that to ask. Too embarrassed of the fact that I had to ask. Every time I thought about it, the layers of shame felt like sweaty, smelly sickbed sheets smothering me. It had seemed like we were dating but then we stopped having sex at some point during the pregnancy and never started again. My body had turned on me, bloated and then cut open and full of infection. And then Cam started hanging out with, and I guess dating, Ben, right in front of my face and she acted like it was nothing so I acted like it was nothing. There was a point when I think it would've made sense for me to say something but that point passed because I was terrified to have to ask, to have to say, "Aren't we dating?"

And then I was embarrassed that I was too weak to ask. Sometimes I thought of our connection as deeper than all that, deeper than stupid high school dating, we were like family, but that wasn't quite right either. Did other people just know when they were dating or did they say it, in words, out loud? I'd never been good at saying things out loud. It felt like I missed the part where they taught us that. Like in class when everyone else knew how to do the algebra equations and all I had in my mind was a blank space.

The truth is I didn't talk to Cam about Ben or our relationship because I couldn't talk to her about how she was changing. I wanted so badly to avoid the things I didn't understand, to rush right over any discussion of what she was doing. Even though I'd given her hormone shots and read the pamphlets, I didn't really ask. I didn't really listen. I had thought of our relationship as just a different version of what Mom and Daddy had: high school love bleeding into long-term dependability. A relationship where not much needed to be said. I loved Cam and I thought that was enough. I didn't think I had to talk about love to make it real. I didn't understand her transition really but I understood that I loved her. Of course, I didn't say any of that. What I hated most about Ben was how easily he talked to Cam. I had thought of the momentum of us as bigger than any words.

Mom was still looking at me. Cam was still standing in the parking lot. I turned away from the window and looked at Eva, who was happily smashing a pile of mashed potatoes with her tiny fist.

"I gotta go pee," I said.

When I got back, Cam was walking in the front door. She plopped down in the booth beside me, exhaled loudly.

"He's not coming," she said and leaned forward, her hair hiding her face. "There's some senator he was supposed to meet with today who rescheduled for tomorrow so he's staying in DC."

From the highway overpass outside I heard a squabble of car horns and sirens.

"Well, Eva doesn't know the difference," Mom said after

the silence had stretched for a while. "She doesn't know what day it is."

Cam looked up. "Yeah, but I do."

I watched Eva patty-caking the mashed potatoes. I wished I hadn't gone to the bathroom before. I couldn't think of any other excuse but I couldn't stay at the table.

"We'll celebrate again tomorrow," Mom said. "Tell Mr. Ben this is the only time he's gonna get away with this. By her next birthday she'll know what the word means and we won't be able to just switch it up."

Cam shook her head. "I can't ask you to drive all the way up here again tomorrow. Forget about it, whatever."

"No I figured we'd stay," Mom said. "If you've got a little room in your freezer for the frozen stuff I bought, I figured we'd have a sleepover and then a do-over tomorrow once Ben gets back."

Cam's face cramped in a way I'd maybe never seen before. "No, no," she said.

"Yes," Mom insisted. "Come on, it'll be fun. We'll watch a movie tonight. Maybe something Disney. Eva can watch, too. When's the last time you watched *Fantasia*?"

Cam's face looked like she was being strangled.

"Are we done here?" Mom said. "Or did either of you want another round at the buffet?"

I didn't say anything. Cam didn't say anything. I was watching her closely, trying to imagine what was fucking her up so bad. Maybe Ben wasn't coming back tomorrow? Maybe he'd broken up with her? My heart did an involuntary flip.

"No, Donna, you can't stay," Cam said.

Mom froze, her cup raised halfway to her mouth. "Well why not?"

Cam closed her eyes and then opened them. "Shae's not allowed in the condo. I promised Ben I wouldn't let her come in."

The room shrank to a small spotlight that was only illuminating Cam's lips over and over again: *Shae's not allowed in, I promised Ben, Shae's not allowed in.*

"Well why in the world did he make you promise that?" Mom said.

Cam shook her hair out of her face and looked right at me. "You stole his belt buckle last time you were here."

I felt like I'd swallowed the belt buckle. It was there, cold and solid in my throat. A silver rectangle with an old-timey train. But of course the belt buckle wasn't in my throat, it was in my closet at home. It wasn't like I thought it was worth anything. I'd just needed to take something from him.

My heart was beating all funny. I couldn't look at anyone but Eva. I pushed a plate with a cube of red Jello toward her. I pushed it like I was offering it to her but then I just kept moving my hand until my fingers were inside it, squishing the red gelatin and whipped topping. Eva let out a squeal and grabbed my fingers through the Jello. She squealed again and smiled real big.

"Okay, alright," Cam said and we all looked up, even Eva did. "How about I just come down to Render with you all tonight and tell Ben he has to come there tomorrow to celebrate?"

My stomach and heart reversed places. My blood was moving too fast in my veins. Mom loved it, too. Her face beamed.

"That's a great idea!" she said. "Rodney's supposed to get home tomorrow night, too. We should have a cookout. Oh, I wish I'd known when we were at Costco."

We cleaned the table up as best we could and left the waitress a big tip. Eva was sugar high and coo-singing and then crying. We drove over to their condo, and I nursed Eva while Cam ran in to pack a bag. When she came back out, Mom told her to sit in the back with me and Eva.

"But then you'll be all alone up front," Cam said.

"I'm not alone," Mom said. "We're all together."

EVA WAS SNORING sweetly by the time we stopped for gas. When Mom went in to use the bathroom, Cam turned to me.

"I can't believe that motherfucker," she said. "Costco honey!"

Eva's car seat was between us and we were whispering over it.

"Are you gonna tell Jonas?" I asked.

She looked away out the back windshield. "I don't know," she said.

"Someone should tell him, or tell his mom at least," I said, but what I really meant was someone should've told me. Back when Ben first started coming around Eden's and flirting with Cam. Someone, Jonas maybe, should've warned me. I tried to push my rage away from Cam, to throw it all on Ben, but sometimes I looked at her and felt it sharpening slowly in me like a blade.

It was dark by the time we were approaching Beckley. The radio station we'd been listening to went all staticky.

"Let's play the road-sign band-name game," I said, glancing at Cam. She had taught me the game but it was hard to see her expression in the dark and I suddenly felt enormously stupid for proposing it.

"What's that?" Mom said.

"*Q*," Cam shouted, pointing out at an exit that said Quail Ridge. "Queens of the Stone Age."

"Oh!" Mom said. She loves a good word game. "*F*. Flying Burrito Brothers!"

"Tamarack. *T*. Thin Lizzy," Cam shouted.

"*R*." Mom pointed. "Ricky Martin."

"No solo acts that use proper names," Cam said.

"Oh, come on, that's not fair." Mom was laughing. "Shae," she said, "you gotta get faster, you haven't got one in yet."

I was terrible at the game.

"Next round we should do movie titles," Mom said.

"Deal." Cam nodded.

I pointed at the sign that said Nash's Run. "*N. Neutral Milk Hotel.*"

"Milk what?" Mom said.

"Neutral Milk Hotel."

"A milk hotel? What kind of name is that?" Mom was laughing.

"Well, what about a flying burrito brother?" Cam said.

Mom was caught in one of those laugh-loop cycles. She could hardly get a breath in. It was making Cam and me laugh, too. I felt like I might pee if I laughed too hard.

"At least those are real things, burritos and brothers," Mom said. "What's a neutral milk hotel?"

Cam grabbed her phone from her pocket and opened Spotify. Jeff Mangum's voice droned out into the dark car. *I love you, Jesus Christ.*

"What's that?" Mom said.

"A neutral milk hotel."

"It's Christian?" Mom said.

"Yeah." We were all the time telling Mom that everything we listened to was Christian music but here was Jeff Mangum really crooning about Jesus Christ.

"Why's he sound so weird?" Mom said.

The road signs grew scarce on the far side of Beckley and Cam kept "The King of Carrot Flowers" on and soon we were all singing along, even Mom, and Eva sort of, mumble-whining with us.

"And on the lazy days the dogs dissolve and drain away."

We were driving down Sandstone Mountain into the dark, the mountains rising all around us, our headlights small and burrowing, and we were huddled there together, hurtling through the night as one—and though I knew it was only temporary, I knew tomorrow we would wake up and it wouldn't be the same—but just then, for that moment, it tasted real and sweet.

8 | G-LOC

I knew Mitcham from Ballew's. I knew the general things everybody knew about him: he'd been in the Air Force, he spent a long time in Texas, he'd gone crazy and mistook himself for God.

Mitcham was probably forty or fifty years older than most of us in the basement bar but he liked it down there. And we liked him. Before that spring, I'd never been inside Ballew's. I'd only seen it from the road where it looked like any old shack but stretched out long with no windows. Around back it was stilted on the hill overlooking the river and there were three levels and three decks, each one looking more and more like it was about to topple into the current. Up top there was video poker, in the middle you could get food and stuff, and the bottom bar opened at eight a.m. and stayed open past two if you got the right bartender.

There was a little poison ivy path you could take from the road down and around to the bottom deck. I mostly only hung out there because they didn't care about your age if you came in through the back. Half the bottom level was a store-room with a big sliding padlocked door and if the cops came they just shoved the underaged in there. Same with serving after hours or serving on Sundays. The cops always entered up top and made their way down floor by floor, which gave us plenty of time to hide. One afternoon a bunch of us got locked up in there and the bartender forgot about us. Somebody used a lighter and found the Jack Daniel's.

That day when I was hanging out with Mitcham I was still kinda new to Ballew's. I could name mostly all the regulars and they knew me at least by face, but I wasn't really one of them yet. My time in their world was still short and I was just becoming visible to them. Two years back I was the chubby fifteen-year-old daughter of a cafeteria cook who took the bus from Greenbrier East to Render Elementary every day to eat leftover pizza and help her mom prep for French-toast-stick and hash-brown-patty mornings. But risking your body makes it more valuable. The worse I got into that shit, the more special I became, until I was burning incandescent down in that basement bar. We'd all done terrible things. And it was those terrible things that made us glow. That spring I was still learning everybody's deeds. You couldn't ask outright. And I was still accumulating. The fact that Eva existed and I was there at Ballew's was my main one.

On this particular afternoon, Mitcham had got word that a guy he knew over in Smoot had a bunch of Perc 30s waiting for him. Mitcham got a big government check every month and he always had something on him or in the works. He needed transportation and that's where Jason Hicks came in. But Jason's car was out of gas. I said I'd hitch up the road and bring back a can if they'd let me join.

It must've been late May, one of those days when the sun makes it seem like summer already until suddenly all the strength is gone. They'd cut my Oxy script at my last appointment. I didn't care. I had some definite Percs in my near future. I'd slammed a Jack just before walking up to the road and I could feel it all in me. I could feel my tits perky, my hair blowing like angel-light all around my face. Even the fact that Daddy's half-brother Billy was the one who picked me up couldn't fuck with my buzz. I didn't listen to his judgments. I watched the trees whip like glory past the window of his truck. He asked about Eva. When he said her name, I saw her face for minute, flashing in the sycamore trees. Now that I didn't have a script, I had to get my pills wherever I could and that meant I was out of the house more. I tried to make it home in the evenings and dodge Mom's questions so we could all just sit together and watch the slick color buzz of the TV.

I told Billy to drop me at the Dollar General.

The Dollar General didn't have a gas can, so I had to go across the street to the Family Dollar. Even that didn't fuck with me. I was getting an extra high off how capable I could be and I was back at Ballew's with a big red canister in less than an hour.

Jason and Mitcham were out on the back deck, staring at me. There were a couple of other people there, too, Ditro and Natasha. I didn't know Natasha too well but I liked her. Three months later I would follow her up onto Flat Mountain where she would die but I didn't know a thing about that yet.

"Thanks," Jason said. He took the gas can in one hand and grabbed the belt loop of my cut-offs with the other. He tugged for a second and then let his hand fall down my leg. Mitcham was watching, his lip sliding into a smile.

All my pregnancy chub was gone and all the teenage fat from before that was gone, too. The Oxys took care of it. But I didn't really notice. When I did think about it, I wondered how I looked to Cam. The thing about fucking somebody as pretty as Cam first is that afterward nobody else seems like a challenge.

Jason had an old blue Pontiac. Mitcham got the front seat. I sat in the back with his dog. We drove up Route 12 and the sun reached in and blessed us. The creek gushed by outside the open windows and Mitcham's dog smelled like childhood.

We didn't even make it to Asbury before the Pontiac started smoking. A gray pillar blew up from the hood and then rolled back, covering the windshield and leaking in all around us. We couldn't see out the front and then suddenly we couldn't see anything at all. I couldn't see the dog beside me. Mitcham and Jason were yelling. We rocked to a stop and I opened the door and pushed the dog ahead of me, coughing and crawling in the direction I figured the ditch would be.

"Shit, motherfucking goddamnit, fuck," Jason yelled.

I kept ahold of the dog and stayed low until I could see: Jason hopping up and down, trying to open the hood but it was too hot to touch; Mitcham walking up the road.

We tried hitching but it was useless. Any one of us alone could've got a ride, especially me, but the three of us plus a dog—it was hopeless. I offered to go on my own but I don't think Mitcham trusted me.

"It's only a few hours walk if we cut up over the far end of Keeney." He was looking off across the fields toward the mountain, a soft green slump turning blue in the shadows.

We left the Pontiac still smoking and took off down Blaker Mills Road. Mitcham's dog ran on ahead of us, delighted. He chased a squirrel into a tree, barked at a tractor and circled back to hurry us up. The whiskey I'd had at Ballew's had worn off and I hadn't had any pills since the morning. I was starting to feel real bad, a weak-sick sweaty achy feeling. Jason fell behind pretty quick and I could feel his eyes on my ass cheeks. I was glad we were taking little back roads. Lately Mom had taken to calling the cop shop. McCarty is her second cousin and if he was on duty and things were slow, he'd drive around looking for me. Mostly we just talked, me and McCarty. His cruiser smelled like egg salad sandwiches and he said all the things everyone always said. He knew it must be hard but I had my whole life ahead of me. For Eva's sake, he said, and he pronounced her name like a prayer. For Eva's sake. Eva. Eva. After a while, he'd drive me home.

Cam was worried, too. Funny thing was, when I had enough pills, I could actually act normal and not worry everybody. When I still had a script, I didn't have to run all over the county like a junkie. I'd just take a few to balance me out and I'd be happy at home with Mom and Eva and sometimes Cam. But now I didn't have a script and what I could get at the club wasn't cutting it. Sometimes I couldn't even get myself balanced out enough to go to the club. The tilt came fast and without the script the game was different—desperate, obvious.

Cam had started leaving me worried messages. *Checking in*, her texts said. I hardly read them. And her voice messages bloomed at the bottom of my screen. I never did open them. I wonder if they're still out there, her voice in the cloud. Of course, I can't have a phone here so I don't know that I'll ever hear them.

One time when McCarty dropped me at the house, Mom had a preacher waiting for me. Nephew of a lady she worked with. He was just past pimples, his skin still pocked in places, home on break from Bible college. We sat in the front room, all of us quiet while McCarty backed up and drove away.

Preacher's suit was a stiff new suitcase blue. He opened his mouth.

"No temptation has overtook you . . ." he said.

Eva bounced on Mom's legs.

" . . . .that is not common to man. God is faithful and he will not let you be tempted beyond your ability and after you have suffered a little while . . ."

Out the window a blue jay sat screaming.

". . . the God of all grace, his eternal glory in Christ, will restore, confirm, strengthen."

I watched his lips, soft and pink. He was almost pretty. I wondered what it would be like if he came into the club. It was harder to dance for pretty men. I had to think about myself then, what I really looked like to them.

"The night is far gone," he said, "the day is at hand. So then let us cast off the works of darkness and put on the armor of light."

He was leaning forward, Bible shifting on his knees, trying to catch my eyes. I started giggling, thinking about me thinking about him in the club. I couldn't quit giggling.

"A woman without self-control is like a city!" he said, spit flying from his lips. "Broken into and left without walls!" He was shaking. He lifted his hand and I saw blood, the preacher's wife against the screen, a red ring around her head like Jesus' crown.

I looked to Mom but she wouldn't meet my eyes. I stood up.

"Be sober-minded," the preacher screamed, "be watchful. Your adversary, the devil, prowls around like a roaring lion, seeking someone to devour!"

I pushed my way out the front door and into the pine trees where the blue jay's voice rang free. I tried to call my laughter back but it wouldn't come to me. *Devour, devour!* The jay was as blue as the preacher's suit. *Devour, devour!*

I came back home after dark and lifted sleeping Eva from her crib and held her to me. Mom never mentioned the preacher again.

"WE'RE GONNA NEED to keep moving," Mitcham said.

By the time we'd reached the Blue Sulphur Pike, Jason and I were both out of breath.

"Come on," Mitcham said and he gave us each a handful of fen-phens.

"Hey, I didn't know you could still get these." Jason turned the little capsules over in his hand.

Mitcham shrugged. "You know about Traveller?" he said.

We thought Traveller was a drug but it turns out he was a horse.

"Raised right here. Confederate warhorse. Sixteen hands," Mitcham said.

We cut through Traveller's field and all of a sudden there was a roof out there at the bottom of the ridge. A roof but no walls, just pillars sprouting up out of the grass. Jason stopped to look at it but Mitcham kept on walking.

"Bathhouse," he said.

I stopped, too. It looked like we'd walked back in time. This curved roof and old-fashioned pillars and nothing else around on any side but grass and trees and briar snarls. Up on top of Keeney the clouds had started piling and billowing into a huge blue tantrum. I watched them move at a terrific speed. Inside me I could feel the fen-phens simmering up the way a laugh begins little then builds and spreads through you. We were all of us hooked on Oxys and Roxis and Percs but sometimes an upper was pretty good, too.

I spread my arms and the wind was wanting to carry me up onto that old fancy roof and then up onto the top of Keeney.

"I'm the Queen of the Triple Z!" I called. I didn't know what it might mean but my voice sounded pretty.

By the time I'd caught up with Mitcham, the rain was lashing us and I had so much skin suddenly and nothing really to cover me. The wind was heading in every direction, but mostly it seemed like it was coming straight up from the earth. Jason's pills must've kicked in, too, because he came running past us real fast.

"Shit goddamn it's fucking cold," he said and kept running off the edge of the hill.

I followed and when Jason found a hollow tree, I ducked into it with him. The top was blown off, really only a husk left, but the rain and the wind were mostly outside. Jason was grabbing me and I was swatting at him, reaching over and gathering handfuls of old leaves. I was gonna make us something like Adam and Eve wore. Everybody was gonna be so proud of me.

Then we heard Mitcham hollering. "Good way to get yourself killed."

We looked at the hollow wood all around us, burned black. Lightning likes to strike twice.

"Move faster," Mitcham said. "You'll warm up."

IT WAS ALMOST dark by the time we were halfway up the slope of Keeney, everything covered in purple-blue-gray. I started thinking about how, behind the clouds, the sun was still setting. It didn't stop just because we couldn't see it. Inside that gray mass there was a multicolored sunset happening right at the same time. Thinking about that made me feel less funny about being up on a mountainside in a wet T-shirt and flip-flops while Cam was who the hell knows where.

The darker it got, the more the cold settled into me, and I could barely walk, my body just one big shiver. The rain had let up a little but our feet were sliding on the wet leaves and we were all moving slow, even the dog. Mitcham was way up ahead. I could only just barely make out his shape.

"Hey," Jason called up the hill. "Shae's cold."

"She ain't hardly wearing any clothes," Mitcham pointed out.

I could hear his feet in the leaves as he kept walking.

"Ain't nothing wrong with that," Jason said.

We were working our way up the steep part of the hill then, so steep I had to grab on to little trees sometimes in order to not fall back down. Eventually I just let myself fall. Jason sat down with me. Mitcham's dog ran circles back and forth between him and us and I was tracking his movement until after a while I saw an orange light up ahead.

"Come on," Mitcham called.

It was a flame. When we got close enough, I could see that Mitcham was gathering the dead lower branches from the bottoms of the pine trees, the ones that were sheltered from the rain.

"Warm up and dry out," he said and handed me a couple of more fen-phens.

I swallowed and stood before the fire, arms stretched, turning slowly. Our shadows twitched against the hill.

"Hell, I'd go ahead and throw myself across the top of a lightning-struck tree if I thought it would do any good," Mitcham said, coming in with another armful of branches. "At this point though I'd say my body's a death-deterrent."

"How's that?" Jason asked.

"I've tried so many times."

"How come?"

I watched them, quiet. I always like it when other people ask the questions.

"We switched places up there," Mitcham said, prodding at the fire. "Now I'm in the wrong me and since they won't let me in the cockpit and they won't let me back in the centrifuge, the way I see it, we won't meet again till death."

"Who's we?" Jason was looking at Mitcham and Mitcham was looking at the fire. I shivered. There was a chill on me now bigger than just the cool of the evening. Despite all the drugs we did, most of us who hung out at Ballew's tried to keep ourselves at least partially tied to what everyone else called reality. We tried to stay close to the doorway so we could step back in any minute. But Mitcham's words weren't stringing together right and he had a look in his eyes like it didn't even matter. He'd let go of the edges of reality, and now, like a sheet too small for the mattress, it wouldn't fit no matter which way he pulled.

"Him and me," Mitcham said.

"Who's him?" Jason asked.

"The other me."

Jason made a sound halfway between a snort and a laugh.

"It wasn't till I started working with Whinnery that I saw him. It wasn't till I blacked all the way out. But they started me working with Whinnery because I *wasn't* blacking out."

"What were you on?" Jason asked.

"No, not like that, it's the Gs," Mitcham said. "You ever been on a rollercoaster? You feel the skin on your face suck back? Acceleration and gravitational forces. But that's only about two Gs on a ride like that. And I was pulling up to seventeen Gs when I was working with Whinnery. They picked me because I could stand it."

Mitcham was going down his own memory road now and he didn't care if we came along or not. I stepped in closer to the fire, and the warmth was like its own drug. I closed my eyes and listened to his voice.

"G-force induced loss of consciousness. G-LOC. He'd strap me into this centrifuge. I'd start feeling the Gs and then the tunnel vision would come on and then all of a sudden I'm back home. I'm in the hallway of my house and my wife, I can hear her in the kitchen and I start going down the hallway—only the weird thing is, I'm floating, my whole body is just floating, not touching the ground at all, just hovering over that blue flowered linoleum. Then I turn the corner into my little girl's room and I can see her sleeping in her crib, her black curls are sweaty and she's sucking her thumb. But there's this other guy there, too, leaned up on the crib, watching her. He reaches out and brushes her curls and that's when I see it's me down there. And of course, you gotta ask, if that's me down there, then who's this up here, right? But that's just when Whinnery shuts off the centrifuge. He says I was blacked out for fifteen seconds. Sixteen Gs. I told him send me back up."

I looked at Mitcham and his face was so full with it. *Send me back up!* It was terrifying and naked and beautiful and I knew I was there, too, strapped into something too big to let me loose.

"When I got back," Mitcham said, "my baby girl was alone and the other me was in the kitchen with my wife. Every time I got in close to where I mighta been able to touch Him,

Whinnery would shut off the centrifuge. I kept going for it. I couldn't get Him to look at me though. He was carrying on with my wife and my kid. I thought if I could get Him to look me in the eye, if I could touch Him, we'd trade back and I could get inside my life. I couldn't do it though, there was never enough time." Mitcham stepped in closer to the fire and kicked the sticks with the toe of his boot. "My wife, she wouldn't look at me neither. I'd be floating there and she wouldn't even look at me. I'd get out of the cockpit at the end of the day and I'd call her on the phone and tell her He's not me. Don't let Him touch you like that. She wouldn't listen."

Mitcham looked up and his eyes were breathtaking. Something so huge I couldn't look away.

"Well, shit," Jason said quietly and then there was nothing but the sound of Mitcham's dog snuffling in the leaves. I felt a prickle travel up my arms. I started thinking about another me watching me from above and behind. All that spring and summer I kept telling myself I was gonna kick the Oxy and clean myself up. Soon, soon. I was gonna quit before Eva was old enough to remember. That way she'd never know I hadn't always been there with her. I'd cancel out this me sitting up here on the mountainside with my brains razzed out with a me that had never left her side. If she didn't remember it, it would never be.

The fire popped and spat. There was a me at home with Eva right then, watching *BoJack Horseman* while she slept. I just had to get back. I had to crawl inside that me and hold on.

"Alright," Mitcham said, "let's go."

We staggered in the dark, running into tree branches and sticker bushes, and finally when we came over the top of the ridge there were lights down below. A string of moving beams. Pale white and yellow. Enormous glowworms inching and stitching. I turned to look for Jason and Mitcham but all I saw was the dog. I froze up and sat down. I couldn't move toward them and I couldn't look away.

"Road work," Mitcham said and suddenly they weren't glowworms at all. But they were still beautiful. I could hear the deep thrum of motors down below. The curve of I-64 between Smoot and Meadow Bluff.

"Come on, girl," Mitcham said, but I couldn't move my legs. He took my outstretched hand in his and his fingers were warm and strong and calloused.

"I like this you," I said.

He shook his head but he let me keep holding on to him as we stumbled down into the valley.

We must've got our Percs that night though I don't remember much of it. I must've seen Mitcham again after that night, too, but I can't remember anything specific. I just remember that newspaper photo of him right before they put him away. I just remember that he was smiling. They ran the picture on the front page of the *Mountain Messenger* and in it Mitcham's handcuffed but he's grinning like a baby.

He'd rented the apartment right next door to the Render Pharmacy, it was later that same year. Pills were real hard to come by on the street. He started tunneling into the duct system. When he realized he was never gonna fit, he paid a kid to shimmy through the pipes, drop through the air vent, and open the door for him. McCarty was on patrol that night and he saw a flashlight in the pharmacy.

Now Mitcham's up at Huttonsville. I asked the new nurse here about him. I know she was transferred from there. I know, too, we're not supposed to ask about inmates and I know they train the nurses not to listen, but I swear I saw her eyes perk up when I said his name.

9 | RED CARPET

It was because of Ben that I ended up at the Red Carpet Lounge on a Tuesday night right after the Fourth of July. He'd forgiven me. I was absolved and allowed in his condo again. The belt buckle I'd stolen was back in its rightful place. I was doing better. I'd balanced myself out enough to work a good stretch at the club and buy myself enough pills to act normal again. Mom drove me and Eva up to Charleston on Monday and said she'd be back to pick us up Wednesday afternoon. Until things turned bad on that Tuesday night, everything was going real good. Ben made homemade pizzas. Cam was taking a summer class, something in science. I helped her study while Ben cooked. It all felt steady. I gave Eva a frozen plastic ring. She was teething. I held Cam's flashcards in my hands and they wove me into everything.

"A bond where electrons are transferred?"

"Ionic."

After Eva fell asleep, we watched a movie that Ben chose. *Wild Hearts Can't Be Broken.* I was all prepared to pass out, I'd swallowed an extra Oxy after supper. But the movie was better than I expected. Mom would've really liked it and I wished she were there, too. It was a love story but mostly between a girl and her horse. Usually, I hated those type of girls, like the ones we'd gone to school with, their shiny hair and riding boots, but this one was fierce. She rode her horse off forty-foot towers and dove all the way down into a swimming pool. She went blind and kept right on doing it. I guess she was either fearless or stupid.

The next day Eva and I ran errands with Cam and I could see the shape of her days—the campus at the University of Charleston, the teacher who waved her down to talk about some upcoming class, the bookstore café downtown where they knew her by name. I carried Eva on my hip and everywhere we went everyone knew she was Cam's—same hair, same eyes, same lips—a little piece of Cam I'd somehow made inside myself.

Cam asked about my days, about work, and I told a story I'd been saving for her. The story of Paul and his letters. According to Raven, Paul had been coming into the strip club for as long she'd worked there. But he only came once a year, on his birthday. The first time he showed up, it took him a while to get around to what he wanted. He'd asked Peggy for a dance but then told her to stop, said the movement made him nervous. He told her he had something in the car he wanted to show her, which of course sounded terrible. But what he brought inside was just a shoebox full of cards and letters. Peggy thought he couldn't read but it wasn't true. He could read just fine. What he couldn't do was deal with feelings. He saved up all the cards and letters his mom and sisters had sent him and got Peggy to read them out loud and write back little responses—*Thank you, I love you, God Bless.*

Peggy quit working at Southern X-Posure right before I started and when Paul came in for his birthday, he chose me. It took all night but he paid good. We both smoked and I read about his sister Jennifer's morning glory flowers and his mother's rotten tooth, his cousin's miscarriage and the baby chick born with an extra foot.

I knew Cam would like that story and she did.

"It's weird but I get it," she said. "It's a lot, letting somebody love you."

BEN SAID "'TACO TUESDAY!'" when we got back to the condo and he started laying out all these different bowls with toppings in them. Then he started talking about hydrologic modeling and epidemiological analysis. Some scientist he knew of from Yale who was doing water studies in Wetzel

County. I couldn't understand anything he said. I picked Eva up out of her playpen but she got fussy so I put her back.

"Robert says they're short-staffed, not enough students signed up, I guess," Ben said to Cam. "Anyhow, I could introduce you and I swear I think they'd let you join."

Cam looked at him across the dining room table. "I don't know if I'm ready for something like that," she said.

Ben pushed it for a little while but after Cam changed the subject and asked me if I'd seen the new *True Detective,* he dropped it. When Cam cleared our plates and carried them into the kitchen, Ben turned to me.

"Talk to Cam for me please," he said. "This is such a great opportunity."

"The Yale thing?" I said.

"Yes."

"You really think they'd let him join?"

I never messed up Cam's pronouns. Okay, well maybe not *never*, but almost never anymore. It kind've made me love Ben to see how angry he got. But it took my brain a second to catch up and realize what I'd done and by then he was yelling about pronouns and assumptions that Cam wasn't good enough. He had so many words, floods of them, so confident and pointed.

"I didn't mean . . ." I said.

"Didn't mean what?"

"I didn't . . ." I couldn't catch enough air to get anything else out.

Cam was in the kitchen with the radio on. In the pass-through window I could see bits of her, moving from fridge to sink. The NPR voice spread loud, lacing in with Ben's words. I couldn't catch any words myself. I couldn't catch my breath. My face turned hot and my hands trembly.

"I fucking love her," I screamed.

Ben's face rippled. "Oh, really?" he shouted.

Cam came around the corner then, her eyes big. "What's going on?"

Ben laughed. He laughed and shook his head. "Well, Shae loves you, apparently, but she can't get your pronouns right and she's pretty sure you're not smart enough to work with the team from Yale."

I jumped up. I did not want to hear any more words. I did not want to see Cam's face.

I ran to the bathroom. With the fan on high I couldn't hear whatever it was Cam and Ben said about me. I had Oxy in my pocket I'd been planning on taking after supper. I was trying not to snort them too much at that point. Snorting them gave me a big beautiful high right away but it also meant I ran through them real fast. Like I said, I was trying not to snort them, but right then I needed it. If I could get to feeling better, then I could go back out and apologize or something.

I had two pills crushed up on the edge of the sink when I heard footsteps.

"I'm sorry."

I was real surprised to hear Ben's voice.

"Shae, I'm sorry, I overreacted."

I bent over the sink.

There was a sound that must've been the door opening. Maybe I hadn't closed it all the way. I don't know really. I didn't look up until I was done snorting.

"What are you doing?" Ben said. "Were you just snorting coke in my bathroom?"

"No," I said. "It's just my prescription." I didn't know if he knew my prescription was gone or not but it was the only thing I figured I could say.

"Your prescription? Jesus fucking Christ. Cam! Cam! Come here right now."

I was blocked in so I looked up at the fan blades. I could feel the Oxy move in me warm and soft, glowing the edges of everything. Ben was yelling and then Cam was there but I focused on those fan blades turning.

"I want her out of my fucking house now," Ben said. "She doesn't care about you. She doesn't even see you."

I knew I would have to turn away from the blades eventually but for the moment their movement was everything.

"And now she's snorting drugs in our bathroom."

Cam's hand on my shoulder was gentle but firm. She walked me down the hallway then out the front door into the foyer. I tried to see Eva before Cam closed the door but she wasn't in her playpen.

"Shae," Cam said.

I looked up.

"Oh god," she said. "You're really high aren't you?"

I bit my lip and looked at my bare feet. I shook my head and then I started to giggle and I couldn't stop. In the carpet, my toes were wriggling.

"God, Shae, please."

I looked up at Cam again and her face was lit with pain. It looked like heartbreak. I didn't even know I could make her look that way.

"I . . ." I said but I didn't know what to say.

Cam exhaled loudly. "You can't stay here. I'll go get your shit."

Through the window I could see out to the street where a car was trying to parallel park. They tried the whole time Cam was gone and still they didn't make it.

"Call your mom," Cam said, handing me my phone and setting my bag by my feet.

I giggled. *Call your mom.* Like I was being kicked out of a middle school sleepover.

"You can wait out here until she arrives."

I giggled again.

"Jesus, Shae, are you gonna be okay?"

I looked up then. Cam's eyes were so blue it was crazy. I wanted to say Eva's name but I didn't. I didn't want her to be a part of any of this. I threw Cam a kiss before I opened the door to the street. I knew even then that Ben was good. He was perfect for Cam. He made her happy. I hoped something terrible would happen to me so that Cam would regret this moment into infinity.

"Oh I'll be fine," I said.

When I got outside, the Camry that had been trying to park was stopped at a crooked angle. I walked right up. I felt a genuine connection somehow, the fact that they couldn't park and I couldn't do anything right either. I was still barefoot.

The driver was a man with a fuzzy little mustache. A red-headed woman sat beside him.

"Hey," I said. "Where do you like to hang out?"

They brought me to the Red Carpet Lounge. It was a cinder-block bunker, looked like some kind of maintenance building. As close to a red carpet as any of us suckers would ever get.

The Camry couple had places to go and people to see, so I walked into the bar alone. I had my shoes on by then. It was dark except for the fish tanks along the back wall and video lottery machines. There were three men at the bar. One of them, sitting by himself with a baseball cap on, turned as I walked in and he started smiling. The bartender came down to where I was taking a seat and I could see he was about to card me when the baseball cap man called out, "Tiffany! What are you drinking?"

"Jack," I said. I didn't skip a beat.

The bartender poured and I didn't even have to use my fake ID or pay for my drink. Tiffany couldn't miss baby Eva because Tiffany didn't even know Eva's name.

The baseball cap man liked to talk. He kept on about the rain and training and wait 'til next year and it took me a while to figure out it was fireworks that had him so upset. He was a new fireman and he'd trained to do the fireworks show for the

Fourth of July. But then it rained. He was so worked up about it I almost wanted to give him a hug. I was on my third Jack by then and I'd scooched down the bar closer to him.

"Where do they keep 'em at?" I asked.

"In a shed."

"Well let's go get 'em," I said. I had the distinct feeling that if I could keep up a good enough momentum then misery wouldn't stand a chance of catching me.

"Fuck yes," he said. "I gotta take a piss."

When Mr. Fireworks went to the bathroom there was just me and two other guys up at the bar. They were sitting close together and one of them had an accent that sounded like New York.

"Could you make me a negroni?" he said to the bartender.

"A what?" The bartender glanced away from the TV and then back.

"A negroni."

The bartender squinched up his face. "You talking about some kind of N-word thing?"

"Oh my god no, no, no."

I giggled. The New York guy couldn't quit saying *no*. It was like he was sneezing and couldn't stop. Then I couldn't stop giggling. Everything seemed potentially hilarious to me.

"See I told you," the other man said.

The bartender turned away from all of us.

I bummed a cigarette. Their names were Dustin and James. James was from New York.

Mr. Fireworks never did come back from the bathroom but I found a new momentum. James was looking for a grave. Dustin was looking for coke. He kept checking his phone. Both of them were buying me drinks. It turned out that Dustin's cousins all lived in Lewisburg and some of them had gone to school with me. He felt we had a connection.

After a while a guy in a pleather jacket showed up and Dustin went out to the patio and came back smiling. James and I followed him back out there. When I snorted my line, I kept hearing Ben scream, *Are you snorting coke in my bathroom?* It made me giggle again.

We left the Red Carpet to find somebody named Turtle to drive us up to a cemetery in St. Albans.

"You were in love, weren't you?" Dustin said.

James was kicking a plastic cup ahead of him up the sidewalk. "Not like that."

"He wouldn't have fucked you anyways, you're too skinny," Dustin said.

"Whatever the fuck," James said. "Now he's dead."

We were walking toward the capital building, the dome like a giant golden egg on the horizon. And then we were walking along the river and I was thinking about Cam and Eva and Eva's birthday, the flowers on the bank of the river and her tiny blond head. Suddenly I was walking with two strange men who were fighting about fucking and graveyards and Eva was up on the hill, only a few miles away but completely out of reach. I could feel her sticky hand around my arm, the wet circle of her mouth. It didn't matter if I called myself Tiffany, her warmth and weight were missing from my body.

"Hey, are you all out of coke?" I said.

We huddled for another bump and James pulled a bottle of Canadian Club out of his backpack. I could feel the momentum picking up again. And sure enough, not twenty minutes later, Dustin found his boat.

"Hey," he said, Canadian Club lifted to his lips. "That's my fucking boat."

Down a steep set of stairs at the end of a dock was a white and blue motorboat.

"Fuck Turtle, let's take the boat to St. Albans," Dustin said.

"Dude, that's your boat?" James said.

"Well, it was."

The story was complicated. James and I didn't wait for it. We raced across the backyard behind a three-story white house.

"Shh-shh," Dustin hushed us.

We ran past roses and carefully carved bushes. We were taking the stairs three at a time. *Clap, clap, clap.*

"Shh-shh," Dustin said again but the house was dark inside and out.

Of course, Dustin didn't have the keys. We spread out across the seats and polished off the Canadian Club while he googled how to hotwire. The boat was rocking in the current and if I closed my eyes it really felt like we were going someplace. When I opened them up again the sky had cleared and the stars were visible. I thought of Mr. Fireworks. That's all he wanted was one clear night.

James couldn't hotwire the boat. He looked so sad and his sadness started to bring in all our ghosts. I pushed my body up the bench seat until it collided with Dustin's and then I grabbed his face in my hands and kissed him good. He tasted like cigarettes and whisky and I didn't know what to do if I took my face away so I just kept kissing him. He kissed back and put his hands on my hips, thumb under my waistband. I kept my eyes closed until suddenly James choked. He made a spluttering sound and I opened my eyes and James was looking up at the house. I pulled away from Dustin. There were lights on downstairs and then up. They blinked off and then a woman came out onto the balcony. She was wearing a white robe and had her hair fluffed up and she looked so soft and pillowy. I glanced at Dustin to make sure he could see her, to make sure I wasn't dreaming.

She stood there a long time and she looked right at us. We didn't move. She didn't do or say a single thing. The night was muggy but the river had a breeze and, every once in a while, it caught the hem of her nightdress. The boat was rocking. The same wind was rocking the boat and lifting her dress and holding all of us. I knew she needed momentum, too. You could see it plain as day.

We stayed that way for a long time, centuries maybe. And then James tripped. The empty bottle hit the deck and broke and the sound spread out. I looked over at James, splayed across the seat, and when I looked back at the house there was a man out there on the balcony. Striped boxers and a belly like a big balloon. The woman was still there and she was saying something now. "Hey, Dick."

He moved fast, or we moved slow, or both. He was coming down the stairs to the dock by the time we climbed out of the boat.

"Stop," he hollered. "I'll call the police."

There was a light on the dock now and it blinded all of us.

"Dick!" the woman called. "Ask them what they need."

James grabbed my hand and I was stumbling behind him through the bushes, unable to see, but I knew she was our angel then because of what she said. The sweetest question. It rang downriver and lifted us all up. "What do they need?" she said. "What is it that they need?"

10 | FLAT MOUNTAIN

The first person I had sex with after Cam was Natasha. This must've been late July or August because the cicadas were out, screaming *now-now-now*. The branches were fat with them. They know better than we ever can how fast we're headed down. How little time. They're greedy and it makes sense.

I was still nursing Eva some but my tits had started to dry up. Mostly she was in Charleston with Cam or at home with Mom. Me, I was out with whoever would message me back. The pills were running low. In Hinton they had black tar, but I hadn't tried it yet.

This night though, it wasn't Eva at home and me out in the woods. Natasha had a baby, too. Younger, probably only six months old. And Natasha had a place up on Flat Mountain where she could crash. A big old farmhouse, looked like it was judging us.

I met Natasha at a river party. She skipped rocks with a shimmering strong pitcher's arm and didn't care if I laughed too soon at every joke. She got muddy and her shirt came open in front of everyone and she just pointed up at the full fucking-beautiful moon. She was a Crookshanks. She was a little older than me, probably nineteen to my seventeen. I kept thinking how much Cam would like her. Natasha had a good smile and she really listened. She had a plan for us. We were gonna set up house together with our babies, up there on Flat Mountain.

We drove her car up in the evening, everything glowing smudgy green and the sun taking its time to set. We'd stopped by the Dollar General and bought a bunch of shit, sour cream and onion potato chips, Red Bull and Gatorade. She'd found an outfit for her little boy that said APPLE OF MY EYE. She had a little bit of black tar for us to share that first night and the next day her dealer, Ditro, was gonna come up and sell us more. I hadn't tried heroin yet, but Natasha had.

The lane was all grown over. Driving it was like going into a long green sleeve. Branches smacked the window glass and then, all of a sudden, we rose up into a field and there was the big house, staring straight at us.

I asked Natasha whose it was.

"Mine," she said.

I hadn't had any Oxy all day and I was feeling like shit. I wanted to try the black tar but Natasha said we had to get set up first. We carried the babies in and left her Johnny strapped into his seat, sleeping on the kitchen floor. The electricity had been cut off and squirrels and bats had moved in. Little feet sheered up the walls as we toured. Garlands of spiderwebs like long, lacy veils. Empty shotgun shells. There was still all kinds of furniture though. We pulled the couch and three easy chairs together until they made a rectangular pen for Eva, with blankets and pillows in the middle.

In almost every single room there was a picture of John F. Kennedy. Natasha went around one by one and turned them all to face the wall. She said you can't trust somebody who knows they're that beautiful.

I'd been taking Oxys for over a year but I'd never shot up. Natasha prepped the spoon there on the kitchen counter. The sun was streaking through the trees. The cicadas were still screaming but quieter now. And the katydids were coming.

I watched Natasha, focused and tender with that flame, and I thought of everything that had been made there on that countertop, all the hands going back over all the years, and I was filled with something big and aching.

She did me first. Tied my arm off and lifted it into the dusty light above the drainboard. She blew on my skin and everything slowed. Skin around veins around muscles around

bones. She traced my vein with her fingernail before putting
the needle in. Slowly, slowly she pressed it and then snatched
the rubber tie off.

"Sit down," she said.

And then she was all around me. She came at me in layers of
warmth from all different directions. Waves of heat. Stunned,
suspended, there was nothing unnecessary. I held her face in
my hands and saw it: each lashed hair so finely built, two steps
from ruin. The sunlight slanted across her cheeks, the pores,
her breath, the only thing moving. The light drained down
across the linoleum and sucked out under the metal-frame door
and I couldn't do a thing about it. It didn't matter. We'd found
a way in. Everything headed toward decay and we were going
the other way. We were swimming upstream and it felt great.

I didn't think about Cam. I didn't even think to not think.
I didn't even have to try.

Johnny woke up and we brought Eva in the kitchen and
taught her to kiss him. Kisses on his dimple fists. She was
hungry but my tits were dry. I felt her hunger pulse through
me and when I looked up, Natasha was reaching. She settled
Eva on one side and Johnny on the other. Natasha's breasts
were marbled and magnificent. When the babies latched on, a
humming entered the room, low and deep and good.

I watched the three of them like you watch a fire, eyes
loose, time gone, body pitched forward.

Night came on us after a while. It was breathing in a way
that matched ours: the bullfrog voices like drunk neighbors

calling back and forth, layered over tree-frog peeps and crickets, katydids and god knows what else. The wind was alive in the cattails and milkweed and in the branches up above and we went out to greet it. Natasha knew the constellations and galaxies.

"Worlds and worlds," Natasha said, "it goes on and on and on and on." She dipped her head back and pointed up and Eva repeated, "Mommy," she said, "Mommy, on, on, on."

We put the babies to sleep in a nest of blankets inside the easy-chair and sofa pen, so they wouldn't wander or roll onto the floor. We went into the back bedroom where the blankets smelled like a different season. The metal frame held her body and her body held me. Full, present, no questioning. Her nipples leaked milk and it tasted yeast-sweet.

IN THE MORNING Natasha was gone and all the windows were warped in their frames. There was fuzz growing on the wall, a haze of mildew across the old white. Something was hollowed out in me. I could feel it blooming up, the way that hunger used to surface in Eva's face when she was tiny and we would watch her and see the milk craving push her, whimpering, up from sleep.

There was nobody in the living room. An empty cocoon of blankets beside the couch.

In the kitchen, Eva sat on the linoleum floor below the sink crushing potato chips in her fist.

"Mommy," she said, holding up her hands. And then she opened her mouth again and I could see all her questions, distinct and fiery bright, all the questions she had for me and would have for me forever on and on into the future and now I couldn't plug up her questions with my tit.

Out through the big sink window, I saw a body walking. Natasha among the cow pies. She had Johnny over one shoulder and her hand stretched out in front of her. Eva and I called to her from the porch and she waved her hand in the air and said something I couldn't understand. I put Eva on my hip and walked out. The breeze against my skin, Eva's sticky fingers clutching, I felt it all over my body, raking me. Natasha stood way out on a rise, pressing her cellphone to the sky.

"Can't get a fucking signal!" she said. The wind lifted her red hair.

My cellphone was dead. Natasha plugged ours both into chargers in her car and turned the engine on to juice them.

"God, I hope he doesn't take all day," she said. "I don't wanna get sick."

Her nose was running.

"Let's clean house," she said.

The cupboards were tall and full of mouse shit.

"Here we go, let's do this!" Natasha took a broom to them.

I didn't know then the clock that she was up against. I just knew mine: I needed two Oxy 30s every day or I'd feel like shit: chills, runny nose, aches. If I didn't get at least one Perc or Oxy or Roxi for more than a day I'd go from constipated to shitting myself. I'd never shot black tar before though and I didn't know that Natasha was dragging around that kitchen with a thinning riddle of time between her and that trembling, rioting bodily doom.

The food we'd bought at the Dollar General took up one tiny corner of one cupboard. Natasha put toys in the rest. Eva stood on the counter and helped her. A pink tambourine. A fluffy black bear. SpongeBob SquarePants. Each one was propped up on its own shelf, displayed like they were for sale.

Natasha lifted Eva down and Eva looked at their work. "P'fect," she said.

OUT BEHIND THE house there was a shed with a few moldering hay bales. I didn't see any animals around. The floor was soft with a fine silt, a silky, dark dirt tread on so many times it had turned to talcum. Eva picked up handfuls and let it run through her fists like sand. Everything smelled of work. Machine oil stink and the tang of metal. One whole wall was hung with implements that stirred up names in me. A mallet, a maul, a poleaxe, a foot adze, a drawknife, a glut, and a shaving horse. They were grandpa tools and I wondered again whose place this was. Could've been Natasha's grandparents, though all the Crookshanks I've ever heard of came from the western end of the county. Could've been her dealer told her it was empty up here. The back wall of the shed was filled with bleached skulls in a perfect gradation from coon at the top down through fox and deer and cow.

"Who?" Eva pointed up at them and then Natasha's scream pierced us both.

She was wearing a pair of pink high heels and kicking at the car tire.

"It's dead," she said and kept kicking the tire. "Engine won't turn over."

She kicked again and her heel stuck in the mud on the tire. Her pale foot lifted and just as she bent to reach for the shoe, her mouth opened and a long string of liquid ran all out and down her leg.

"Fuck. Gimme a minute," she said.

I turned away. Bounced Eva. Wondered where Johnny was.

"Fucking shit goddamn motherfucking fuck Jesus Christ. I'm gonna be sick."

She walked past me toward the porch, grabbed onto the lathed wood banister, and vomited again into the front flowerbed, all over the scraggly cabbage roses and daylilies.

"Did you talk to him?" I asked.

"He's down in Render," she said. "Can't come up here yet."

I found Johnny strapped into the back seat of the car and brought him back in the house. We all sat on the kitchen floor together and watched time drip down the walls. No TV. My phone was charged up but it wouldn't load anything. Eva ate more chips and then she got whiny and started crushing them up and throwing them at us like confetti. I put her and Johnny down for naps in the sofa pen. Dust motes floated through slats of light like the whole world had gone and forgotten about us.

I cut the top off an empty Gatorade for Natasha to throw up in. Her tits were leaking and she squeezed the milk into another bottle.

Ditro had quit texting Natasha back. I told her I'd walk out to the road and hitch a ride and go find him. Make him come quick. I didn't really know Ditro that well but I'd seen him around. He'd be at Ballew's or else somebody there would know where to find him. I kinda thought I should take Eva with me. I looked at her there in the nest of pillows, her pink lips fluttering just the tiniest bit and her eyeballs chasing dreams. But Natasha had milk for her when she woke up and I had nothing.

It took me two rides to get to Ballew's because the first to pick me up was Ms. Walkup who'd worked with Mom in the cafeteria three years back. She wasn't gonna take me to Ballew's. It was all I could do to stop her from driving me to Mom's. So I got out at the Dollar General across the street from the Family Dollar. I bought jars of baby food in shining jewel tones, oranges and yellows and greens, and I felt better already. After Ms. Walkup left, I just waited to find a man alone in a truck.

I told the man to drive me to Ballew's. I tied my baby food jars up inside their plastic sack and walked along the path to the back of the bar. The man with the truck followed me.

Junie was working and she flashed me a smile and looked my ride up and down. He wasn't ugly but one of his eyes was a little lazy.

"Bud Light?" Junie said to me.

I shook my head. My ride was buying so I was going straight for Jack. The bar stools were about half full. Danny and Scotty, Justin, Jason Hicks and Old Man Mitcham down at the end.

"You seen Ditro?" I asked Junie.

"Not since yesterday," she said.

My ride and I took two of the stools and I turned to Justin and cheers'ed. He was nursing a Bud and looking gone.

"You seen Ditro?" I asked.

He shook his head but Jason Hicks leaned up and said. "He's s'posed to meet me here."

So I put my baby food jars on the counter where I wouldn't forget 'em, got Junie to give me another shot of Jack and a beer, and settled in to wait.

It turned out my ride was a Wickline. He knew my dad from before Daddy started long-haul trucking, back when he was working out at the Snowflake quarry. This Wickline was younger than Daddy by maybe ten years but he'd worked out there, too, and he was shocked to make the connection. It was like time had gone and doubled over on him. He kept saying, *chubby-cheeked, curly-headed little thing*, talking about baby me. Luckily this connection didn't stop him from sharing his pills. We stepped out onto the deck to smoke and he palmed and swallowed and I asked for some.

It was right around when Wickline's pills kicked in—uppers of some kind—that I quit paying attention to my phone. Up until then I'd been checking it, texting Natasha and Ditro even though I didn't hear a peep back from either one of them. Time slid away down off the deck after a while, washed away in the current. Wickline kept buying me shots of Jack and when I got wobbly he brought me a golden plate of french fries. I fed half of em to the fishes down below and this tickled Wickline who kept saying *chubby-cheeked, curly-headed little thing.* The fishes rose to the surface, spotted and glistening, an ancient, breathtaking breed. I was thinking about Daddy, wondering where he was that day. Omaha, maybe. Wickline knew a song about long-haul trucking. *I've been from Tucson to Tucumcari,* he sang.

IT WASN'T UNTIL Jason Hicks started fussing about where in the fuck was Ditro that I remembered. The sun was low. Neither Natasha or Ditro had answered my texts. Wickline agreed to drive me back up Flat Mountain. He carried my baby food to his truck, nestled in the crook of his arm, and I kept yelling at him, "Careful, don't break it." I could feel my panic edging up.

He took the third steep curve too quick and the back end of his pickup shimmied out and then the wheels weren't touching. We turned over slow, slow, slower and then a tulip poplar stopped us. Wedged the bed there between the bank and the tree.

Neither me or Wickline was hurt much. He got a little glass in his hand and my hip was bruised. He hauled me out and I was stunned mostly. When I quit seeing black spots in my eyes, I made him crawl back down there for my baby food. My phone didn't have enough of a signal to make a call so he started walking back toward town and I started walking the other way, toward Natasha and Eva and Johnny. I kept thinking that Ditro would pass me after leaving Natasha's and I'd make him turn around and drive me back, but I never did see him.

By the time I made it to the house the cicadas had almost all the way quit. I'd sweated out all the alcohol and pills and I couldn't wait for Natasha to fix me up again. The house made a long shadow all the way to the lane and the edges of the shadow were fraying. Natasha's car was the only one there but the yard was torn up with another set of tire tracks.

"Tasha," I called. My feet were hurting from walking so much in flip-flops.

She was in the sofa pen in a nest of blankets, Johnny sucking on one tit, the other one glistening bare. The first thing I noticed was Eva wasn't there. I called her name.

"Hey, Tasha, where's Eva?"

I lurched and stumbled over the arm of an easy chair.

"Hey, Tasha, wake up."

She wasn't sleeping. It was something about the angle of her neck and how her head lay. Then I saw the needle and the spoon, the little bag of black tar on the blanket beside her. I shook her furiously and Johnny lost his grip on her nipple and started to howl. I was disgusted with him.

"She's dead," I told him. "Dead."

Nothing but skin around veins around muscles around bones.

He screamed louder. I took the needle and the bag of tar and put them on the kitchen counter. The house had tilted all shadowy blue. I ran through the rooms calling Eva's name. If I ran fast enough, I felt sure I could reach out and reclaim all the hours I'd been away. I burst out the back door and the ground was a soft green carpet. All I thought about was Eva and Cam. I begged Cam to help me. I begged her to come. Natasha I could grieve later. Johnny would be okay. But Eva, Eva, Eva. I pictured Cam's face and Eva's, Cam's little clone. Blond curls. Pink lips always parted. I fell in the grass and the dew licked my face. I crawled and when I could crawl no more, I looked up and she was counting skulls. Right there around the back of the shed. Chubby-cheeked, curly-headed little thing. Her hand raised, finger pointing. One. Two. Three. The last ray of sun hit the top row and lit the tiny papery frames.

11 ┊ TERMINAL LUNCH

I said, tell me about the buses and that's what he did. Rolling in, he said, rolling out. And I could feel them. The vertigo of all that chrome rumbling past the windows. New York, Chicago, Los Angeles, Miami. Connected. The same tires that drove through Manhattan went slapping down our own Lewisburg streets, paused, and then shot on to even more famous postcard places. But that was 1970, 1980. It didn't even last to 1990. Long before I was born, the bus terminal was dead. The only thing left was the diner. TERMINAL LUNCH, the sign still read. And there were flies on the flypaper, probably been there since 1973. That's when she started

working, she said. He'd been the janitor in the station, cleaned
the buses, too.

They were old now, or seemed that way to me. Gray hair
coiling through her hair net and poking out from under his
cap. Everything seemed old in there, even time itself. Or
maybe not old but trapped. The clock on the wall with only
the second-hand ticking. Everything yellowed with nicotine
and stalled out. Like when the buses quit coming everything
had given up.

"They'll stunt your growth," he told me, but he handed me
a cigarette anyhow. We all smoked together by the back door,
the view of the parking lot smeared through the dust on the
screen, the stink of the grease trap covering everything.

I tried to imagine the ticket counter bustling, departures
and schedules and maps with roads to new lives, new views
of the same moon. I tried to imagine being that connected.
It wouldn't feel so lonely here if I knew the roads led somewhere, if I could point to a ticket and see my own name. Now
though, we weren't here and we weren't there, no oceans, no
buses, no escaping. Which really only made me think about
it more. If the buses came and went each day, I might never
want to go away.

"You ought to eat something," the old man said, dropping
his butt into a Pepsi can. "Come on, Dreama can make you a
grilled cheese."

I'd asked for a drink. I'd come in all wild-eyed, clutching
my fake ID. I should've known not to mention alcohol as soon

as I saw their wrinkled faces, but no bar was open yet so I'd asked for a beer. *We don't sell that here*, he'd said, but they must've seen a flicker of what had just happened in my face. Something about the way they talked kept me there. Kept me from thinking too much about Cam and the courthouse and the judge. I wasn't hungry but I sat on a vinyl-topped stool and spun, listening to the oil hiss in the deep fryer. It had all happened so fast. I'd thought the courtroom would be bigger, like what I'd seen on TV. I'd thought maybe there'd be a jury. It turned out to be just Cam and me and Mom and Cam's lawyer and our lawyer. And the judge.

The old man pushed a plate down the counter. The porcelain rocked and sang. Fries and white bread and yellow cheese glistening. I'd told the old couple that Eva was sick, it was easier than explaining custody. I said she had to go up to Charleston full-time for a while to get better.

Truth was, it happened so fast I was still dizzy. Cam walked in wearing that suit, her hair pulled back slick. I know she must've hated having to dress like that. She looked so capable though—she *was* capable but she looked it then in a way they could see—and she was well on her way to getting a degree.

I panicked when I saw her. *Where's Eva?* I said. I'd always pictured she'd be there, although that wouldn't've been fair. She was with Ben in Charleston. It was a shock seeing Cam in that suit. It felt bad, like we'd stumbled into something violent and wrong, everything about the last two years all twisted and broken and somehow leading us to this moment.

I didn't let our lawyer mention Cam's transition. Mom brought it up in our prehearing meeting but she didn't even know what to say.

"Shouldn't we tell the judge about what Ben told me?"

"What do you mean?" I said.

"Whatever that was that Ben said about pronouns?" Mom was looking at me.

"What's this?" The lawyer put down the piece of paper he was holding and glanced from Mom to me.

"No," I said.

"Pronouns?" The lawyer was looking directly at me.

I shook my head again. "She doesn't know what she's talking about."

The lawyer turned to Mom but Mom didn't say anything.

"It doesn't have anything to do with anything," I said. "I mean, it doesn't have anything to do with whether Cam should have Eva or shouldn't."

It turned out, that wasn't the question anyhow. The question was whether *I* shouldn't. The answer was yes. Then the question was whether Mom shouldn't, and that answer was also yes. *With so many grandparents raising grandkids these days,* the judge said, *it's wonderful to finally find a case where one of the parents is more than ready.*

Dreama brought me a Pepsi and I asked if she didn't have a Coke. They both laughed.

"Well, she's plucky, in't she?"

I watched the windows for buses.

"I can't stay long," I said. "My stop's coming."

Every other weekend. That's what the judge gave me. Or gave Mom, really. I was allowed to be there but it was Mom who got weekend custody.

Dreama decided I should have some milk. She brought me a tall glass with a paper doily. The milk said I was still somebody's baby.

Eva had almost all her front teeth. Perfect cutting pearls. I told Dreama and the old man about them. *Dean.* I don't know if that was his name was or I'd just made it up but it seemed right. Dreama and Dean. I told them how after a while she'd lose those teeth but it was okay cause they'd grow right back. I wondered why more things in life weren't like that.

They really listened to me, Dreama and Dean.

No one else came in to eat and only the second-hand was moving and I'd begun to believe I'd imagined it all—fallen down some rabbit hole—when Dean's cellphone rang. I was so surprised I almost screamed.

"Uh-huh, well, alrighty then, I'll be right up," he said into the cellphone and then to Dreama he said, "Ms. Johnson lost her key."

I hated to leave Dreama but I was afraid I'd never get free if I didn't go with Dean. I needed momentum. I had to grab it by the tail. It seemed my stop wasn't coming and the milk was gonna run out.

Besides, I liked his keys. He had a big round ring of 'em weighing down his jeans. He said we were headed to the old high school. They had social-service type programs there now but the lady who ran it was always locking herself out.

"They've kept me on because I'm the only one can run the furnace," he said. "Big old coal-burning beast."

It was September and warm enough for short sleeves but come evening a chill would set in. We walked up the hill and when I turned my head, I could see the redbrick courthouse through the trees. I wondered how long Mom would wait. I'd left her in the bathroom stall. I'd never done a thing like that but I couldn't take it. I couldn't get back in the car and drive home with her. She'd been so sure we would win and then go get lunch at Food & Friends or Chinese. I'd slipped out of the bathroom while she was peeing. I'd slammed open the emergency door so I didn't have to see Cam. The alarm wasn't any louder than the panic in my brain.

I still remember the first time Mom left me. At my aunt Suzy's house. It couldn't've been the first time really, but the first time I remember. Suzy had this horse that somebody or other was boarding. She'd let Mom ride and she'd watch me. Mom put on boots that smelled different than anything I was used to and she walked out the door and into the field. She walked out of my reach and then she walked on even though I kept reaching. I watched through the window, leaned up against the back of the couch, vibrating with feelings. When I was real little, Mom didn't work, she stayed home with me. But here she was, out there against the trees, doing something that had absolutely nothing to do with me. I was sad, yeah, but it was more than that. Somehow my little brain had begun to realize she was a person separate from me. She had her own wants and needs and feelings and she had a body separate from me. I don't guess I really knew about death then but I could feel it somehow, just how alone each of us finally is.

"It'll be alright," Dean was saying, and when I looked at him funny he said, "Your little one. It could be worse. You could be like these fools." He pointed to the cars running idle in the parking lot. It turned out that the program that was locked out was court-appointed supervised visitation for all the fools who'd lost custody.

We watched them shuffle in. One man had a dinosaur in plastic packaging, he carried it chest-level, delicate and indiscreet. One man had a dozen roses in pink paper and lace. The kids were runny-nosed or dozing, not a one of them wanted to be there.

When we went down to the basement to see the coal-burning beast, Dean pulled a flask from behind the water tank. I was sad and so relieved. I'd wanted him to not have the need. The whiskey calmed me though. Right away I knew I was exactly where I was supposed to be.

Dean opened the basement door and started sweeping, the broom throwing dust particles up into the sun. I listened to the broom. I watched the rays. Time wasn't trapped here but it was still slow. I thought about Cam zipping up the road, trees whipping by as she drove home with her piece of good news tucked inside. But she might have already been in Charleston by then. I had no idea what time it was. I guess I was thinking about time that day because of what Cam's lawyer had quoted. *Oxycodone lengthens reproductions of suprasecond time intervals—shortened time horizons lead to the devaluation of future consequences.* Back then, I had no idea what any of that might mean. There's a doctor here though who comes in to talk to our drug rehab group and he explained it plain. When you're high time is not the same and all consequences feel far away.

Our clocks were running opposite. Cam was racing toward her future, building a world for herself and Eva, a place where she could do more than just survive. I was suspended, floating, gestating. Sometimes I think it started with the pregnancy, even before I had any opioids in my veins. Time stretched and turned thick, near impossible to move through. All I could do was tread in place. Maybe my time intervals have always been funny. Ever since I was a kid, I'd hide in time. My childhood was hazy with praise and contentment. Cam's never even existed. When we met, I wanted to believe I could smuggle her in, open the soft and easy afternoon and pull her under the blanket.

That day with Dean, I could've believed there was no such thing as time. He swept the basement while I worked on the flask. Above us, children's feet shivering.

"Come on," he said after a while. "I don't need to start the furnace for another few hours yet."

We walked through the playground and out to where the blacktop rolled into clay, running red-brown between the fencerows. Dean said he'd been born in a house that used to sit back this way. He didn't say much more and that was okay. I knew I was due to work at the club that night but I couldn't care. I could feel something coming toward me from deep in my own future.

The afternoon was screamingly green. At a glance, it was still summer, thick leaves and goldenrod blooming furiously. But along the edges, fall was coming. Queen Anne's lace already dried to brittle stalks. Dandelions gone to seed. In the face of the oak, I could see her winter form, raw and shook, barely believing. A warm wind threshed the green leaves, but if you knew how to look, they weren't fooling anybody.

12 | ANGEL BITCH

I loved to sit at the back and watch them come in, I loved it when they leaned right up against the mirrors on the long wall and then everything dropped away into that moment—peeking from their bags, you'd see baby formula and community college textbooks, but in the mirror that was gone, replaced by eyeliner, ringlets, tongue at the corner of the lip, and then boom—the music went up and the lights went out and then everything reversed and in the bright silence Raven stood.

I'd missed three, four, maybe five shifts. I was shaky even in my tennis shoes. I needed a fix.

Raven's arms rose up like all the arms I'd ever loved and missed, and her face closed in on me, oxblood lipstick.

"What the fuck kind of place do you think this is?"

In the drop-tile ceiling there were watermarks that looked like piss.

"You think we need your ass that bad? You just stop in whenever you want?"

Kandice wasn't working that night. I searched the room for her anyway. I'd gotten a ride in with Harmony but she was brand new and also conveniently not in the room.

Raven held up a piece of paper. Black Sharpie, bad handwriting. Amie, Angel, Melody, Glory, Harmony, Heidi, River, Skylar, Tiffani, Vivian.

"This is my pussy party, bitch."

I tried to leave through the bar but Raven pushed me out the back door, and when I circled around, the bouncer was jumpy and sad-eyed.

"Raven says—"

"I just need to see if Colton's in there."

He looked down at his rubbery shoes.

"Raven says—"

"Fuck it." I slung my backpack over my shoulder. "Can I bum a smoke?"

Colton's car was not in the lot and he would not answer his phone. Harmony wouldn't be ready to drive back to Render until at least two in the morning.

I started walking away from the club, looking down over I-77 and Princeton. Clouds came pushing up from the south and the temperature was dropping and over to the west the sun was snarled in a heart-grip of fury. The mountains make a bowl here at the very bottom edge of West Virginia and it is easy to see how this was once a coast. The Great Inland Sea, they'd taught me, with the heater ticking and the pages filled with pictures of shells and scales and words I was hungry to pronounce. And I could see it, even there in the warmth of that classroom, I could see it reaching across time, salty and insatiable, followed by giant sloths and mastodons.

By the time I'd made it down to Oakvale Road, it was raining. I didn't know where I was headed but I stuck out my thumb. The rig that picked me up was fire-engine red. His tires sliced an arc of rainwater all across my legs. He didn't ask where I was going, just worked his chew around in mouth and pointed up ahead.

The truck stop was swimming in puddles and neon lights. He got out to pay for fuel and I rolled down my window. I'd tell him how my dad drove long haul for Hardin, I figured that would help. The cab smelled like piss and something sweetly sickening. I looked around for cigarettes but he only chewed I guess.

"Hey," a voice said.

I looked down. She was small as a child there beside the chrome running board, all big hair and dark eyes.

"My husband saw you back there but I didn't 'cause I was

driving. I hate driving in the rain. I always have. I can't get comfortable with it."

Her face was creased and her makeup smudged and thick.

"Come on," she said. "Don't take rides with single men. That's how I ended up with my husband."

I wondered if I was supposed to laugh. I was comfortable despite the bad smell. I just needed to get somewhere where I could score. Wheels under me would get me there for sure, wherever there was.

"I'm not kidding." The woman yanked herself up toward the door. "I won't sleep tonight if you don't come with us."

She offered me a smoke and I followed her. Their rig was around back. I thought one ride was as good as the next, but I realized too late they weren't in any kind of hurry. They weren't even picking up their load until the next morning.

"What the fuck?" I said.

The red rig was gone, spitting rain back onto the interstate.

"Fuck you," I said to the woman who'd introduced herself as Sylvie.

She lit a cigarette and leaned up against the wall of the truck stop.

I called Colton's phone. He didn't pick up. I was soaked through now and working on my pity. I tried to brandish it for myself the way I always had, in full peacock colors, but it was diluted and so I reached for something else. I wanted anger. I thought of Cam up in Charleston. She'd never even asked me if I wanted to move. I tried to fill myself up with hate. I wanted to burn with thoughts of her but mostly I just felt lonely and I couldn't do anything glorious with loneliness.

I looked over at Sylvie. I liked her despite myself. It was her hair. She had big, teased-out hair like my piano teacher, Ms. Bryant. Ms. Bryant's hair had matched her poodle's and I used to wonder how she slept with hair like that. I went to her house for my lessons and once, on my way to the bathroom, I snuck into her bedroom to see if she had a special kind of pillow to help with that stiff halo of hair but there was nothing unusual. The mysteries of the adult world, I could feel them sliding past me like sand. I still do. There is always something everyone else understands before I do.

"Why do you care what happens to me?"

Sylvie looked up. She was one of those holographic women, one moment she looked twenty-five, the next fifty. "Bill said you looked like our kitten."

"A kitten?" I glanced at their rig. I wondered if I would have sex for money.

"He calls her Angel. I call her Bitch."

THE TRUCK WAS pitch dark inside. Sylvie hoisted herself up first and I followed. There was movement and breathing, indistinct and big.

"Shut the fucking door!"

I jumped and the lights came on and flying toward me across the seats was a black-and-white cat.

Sylvie shoved me out of the way and grabbed the door. The cat backed up and spat.

"How many times do I have to tell you to watch the fuck-ing door?"

The man was sitting on the edge of the sleeper cab bed.

"Do you know Rodney Phillips?" I said.

They looked at each other and then at me.

I sat down and the seat hugged me like only one of those big-rig seats really can. I hadn't been inside my dad's rig in years and years. I used to love it. But of course, Dad didn't want to spend his off time there and anyhow he couldn't drive it up to the house so for me to go see it was a special trip.

It was warm inside Bill and Sylvie's rig and it smelled like microwave spaghetti. I wasn't dopesick yet, just shaky and weak feeling, but I knew it was coming. Only a matter of hours. Still, the kitten was purring in the driver's seat and Bill was laughing and waving around a Shrek DVD.

I checked my phone. No calls. No texts.

I told myself, in one hour, Colton would call me. He'd say he was up at the club and he had plenty of Oxys and then he'd drive down the hill and come get me.

In the truck-stop bathroom, I put on Sylvie's sweats. They were pink fleece and only a little bit short in the leg.

We watched *Shrek 2*, all in a row on the bed. They smoked me up and the weed gentled my coming dopesickness.

"Don't worry," Donkey said. "Things just seem bad because it's dark and rainy."

Outside, the Shell sign glittered all wet. Inside, it was impossibly warm and snug and I felt sure that before I was born, Dad had laid beside Mom in his cab just like this and I was there, too, just barely there, inside her, curled and floating in a darkness inside a more perfect darkness. I wanted to stay there forever, to move back away from this life and climb inside that memory. Only it's not true or I'm not sure if it's true or maybe she rode with him once, maybe it made her sick, or maybe she never did, but maybe, just maybe, we were meant to stay there rolling, forever, just the three of us— nothing visible but what we could see through the windscreen, the treeline sky and birds above, everyone else below us, no decision permanent because we'd never arrived yet.

13 ┆ TAMARACK

Sick Sundays. A heartsickness that set in every two weeks. Mom and I would pick Eva up on a Friday evening and drop her off late Sunday afternoon. The ride up on Friday was awkward but not too bad. I didn't know what to say to Mom anymore. She put the radio on 99.5 The BIG DAWG in Country and turned it up just a bit too loud. And then going home with Eva, all the awkwardness was gone. We'd sing songs and I'd feed her snacks from different Tupperwares Mom had fixed.

Eva loved bugs and slugs and salamanders and snails. I took her out into the woods behind the house and we'd turn over stones to find the roly-polies there. She loved the wet tongue of moss at the base of the oak tree and she would press her cheek against it, eyelashes batting. Mom couldn't stand anything crawly but this just made Eva laugh.

"Look, Grandma," she would call and then unfurl her tiny fist to reveal a battered moth or millipede. "Creepy!" she would scream, her laughter coming in fits.

Daddy switched his schedule so he was home on Eva weekends and we'd cook out and watch movies and make blanket forts in the living room. I could hold it together for a little bit. By Saturday evening though, I could feel it coming. We all could. Sunday morning, Mom would cook a big breakfast but none of us besides Eva wanted to eat. I'd slide my sausage links into the garbage along with the runny egg.

It was only an hour drive to Tamarack but we always left early. Mom was scared of getting there late. She was scared of how much Cam and Ben had already taken away. She covered over her scaredness with makeup and games. As soon as breakfast was over, she'd sit down at her vanity and start with the brush, pulling it through her short, permed hair until it puffed up. Eva and I sat behind her on the bed. Eva playing peekaboo and me trying to learn to French braid. Mom changed her eye shadow to match her blouse but she always wore a lip color called Miss Mauve. When she got upset, her hands shook. If she messed up the lipstick, she'd pull out a baby wipe and take it all off. Start again, patiently. Once I watched her do it three times, baby wipe gently caressing the corner where lip becomes skin.

On Eva weekends, I balanced my pills out carefully. I'd go sick other days just to make sure I had enough for those weekends. Enough to keep me steady and just shy of high. Sundays were hard though. Sundays, I wanted to obliterate. I'd wake up with Eva snoring lightly beside me and I'd think about the back door of the sunporch. I'd trace a path in my mind that led to Ditro or Colton and eventually to Ballew's. On Sunday afternoons they always had free food at Ballew's. I wasn't big on eating in those days but I loved the feel of it, Danny and Scotty and Justin tending a big pot of crawfish and Mitcham coming in with a skillet of fried potatoes, Junie taking a break to grab a plate.

But on heartsick Sundays, Daddy would get back on the road and Mom and me and Eva would drive to Exit 45. In the back seat I'd read storybooks out loud until I felt too carsick to see. "Do you like my hat?" "No!!!" Eva crooned, a smile so big it split her face.

It was the drive home that was the worst of it. I'd rather Mom had yelled at me, told me I was a fuckup, failure, nightmare dream. But instead, she didn't say anything. She chewed all the Miss Mauve off her lips and her nails trembled against the wheel.

WE DID THE drop-offs and pickups at Tamarack and when Eva and I went in to the bathroom, we'd see the tourists shuffling around looking at tourist-trap shit. My favorite was a T-shirt with a picture of a bear that said SEND MORE BACK-PACKERS, THE LAST ONES TASTED GREAT! I tried to explain it to Eva but the humor was a little advanced. She liked the plush toys, the dense red down of the state bird. I bought one for her even though it cost thirty-five dollars and I was hardly working anymore.

Ben always came with Cam. From down the parking lot I could see them, Ben's dark hair and Cam's blond. Sometimes you'd see other families, too, and it was obvious what they were doing, backpacks in hand, awkward looks on their faces. *See you next week!* We didn't even get every weekend. Mom was careful, careful, careful with what we did get. She brought baked goods every Sunday, cinnamon rolls or pigs in a blanket. She'd set us up at a picnic table with a roll of paper towels, sippy cup of milk, bib, everything you could possibly need to take good care of a kid. Ben and Cam would join us and I'd wait one long minute and then say I had to go piss. Stretch out that bathroom break as long as it could possibly take.

We ate outside even though it was a little too chilly now, already October. If you sat inside, you had to order food at the Tamarack restaurant. From the bathroom window, over by the hand dryers, I could see our table. I could see Mom pass Ben a paper plate. I could see Eva's laughter reflected in Cam's face. And at the next table over, I could see it, too, a man and a woman and a redheaded boy and girl and the fault lines we pretended did not take up so much space. Up above them all, the sky was shrinking.

I walked out front to the area with all the little brochures for cave exploration and mine museums. I walked slowly, watching, waiting. The sky to my back was still wide open, sending sun onto the tables, but the birds had all gone quiet and the leaves began to quake.

The rain set in before I made it to the tables. A big dip and rise and then a wall of wet wind and hail. Everybody rose all at once, paper plates blew against elbows, hats against faces. I ducked back under the roof by the brochures. A big belly roll of thunder collapsed on top of us. Voices pitched and then muted and everybody got mixed up into it. I lost Cam and Eva and Mom in the scramble. I kept looking for the electric pink of Eva's dress and I remembered a story my grandma told me.

Mom's mom was named Viola and she didn't say much to us kids or show any preference. I don't think she cared much to distinguish one of us from the rest. She'd had eleven kids and worked over at Morlunda Farms until her fingers wouldn't bend enough to make a fist. One day we were stringing beans on her back porch when it started to rain and she told me about a flood that happened when she was a kid, over in Palestine off Blue Sulphur Springs Road. Rain came down hard one afternoon out of a clear August sky, there was so much of it so fast it formed a new river that spilled off the ridge of Keeney and came down the holler where the houses were stacked. It wasn't a *river* river, just a flash stream, but it moved fast and picked up hogs and bedframes. The funny thing was, Viola said, it was choosy in what it took. It was a thin stream for all the power it had and when it wound through a house it would pick one thing and leave another. It took two chicks from a hen's nest and left the other six. It took one of Viola's only pair of shoes, patent leather black with blue flowers embroidered around the lace holes. Viola stood on the table as it raced through and she thought at first it was God laughing at them for valuing all these earthly things, but the longer she thought about it, the more it seemed that the funnier thing was how we could take something as big as the sky and turn it into a lesson pointed straight at each of us— you loved this too much, you loved that, a ballerina figurine, a swan-shaped butter dish. Because we need our losses to make some kind of sense.

14 | HAMMERHEAD

The problem was, he cut too deep. Waited too long and cut too deep. A line so precise even an idiot couldn't mistake it for an accident. Colton and I were on a family visit of sorts, up on Muddy Creek Mountain. Colton's uncle, Luther, kept calling me Little Missus. Either he hadn't seen Colton's wife in so long he forgot what she looked like or maybe he thought Colton had got a new one. I didn't say anything. Luther had a bunch of land, most of it slicked down into rusty mud patches. He had hunting dogs staked to little doghouses, each one with a different design—intricate and mesmerizing. Cupolas and widow's walks and multi-angled roofs. The dogs were rangy and deadeyed. They ran circles around their chains and kicked orange mud up in great sprays against their own personal balconies.

Luther also had a portable sawmill.

"So where is it?" he said.

Colton squinted and slugged the last of his Bud. It was November but real warm out and we were drinking in the yard.

"What?" Colton said.

"Well, I know you didn't just come up here to tell me you love me."

"Huh?"

"You said you had something you needed cut."

"Oh," Colton said, and then he held up his arm.

"So where is it?"

Colton waved his arm. He had a ratty plaster cast.

"Bull-fucking-shit," Luther said.

Colton nodded. "I've done it myself before. Did it with a hacksaw blade but it took fucking forever. Just show me how to run the thing."

"You're gonna lose your fucking arm. End up a janitor."

"Janitor?"

"You remember that fuck-wad that Nina hired to clean the diner at night. One arm."

"He sawed it off?"

"Dirty needles," Luther said. "Over and over in the same vein. Got gangrene."

"See," Colton said. "Now that's just stupid." He grinned and opened another Bud. Colton had a great smile, crooked enough to catch in your stomach and pull up to your heart. "What the fuck ever," he said. "I'll do it myself."

When Luther saw he was serious, he said they'd be better off using a chainsaw. He said he had a lightweight Craftsman.

The saw was in a long shed that smelled of pine. I wandered away to the end of the shed where the light sliced in and framed the wood curls spilled all across the floor, each one perfect and singular. The saw ripped awake and snarled. I picked up a curl and held it cupped in my palm. The saw stopped. The saw snarled. I dropped the curl and watched it spin. The saw stopped. The saw snarled and then Colton screamed. I turned. I thought I'd see a geyser of blood, a horror movie stunt, but there was nothing. The chainsaw was on the floor beside Luther and Colton was dancing backward, holding his cast to his chest. Luther walked over.

"Let me see it," he said.

The cut wasn't deep but it fouled up the plan. The idea was to get the cast off and crush Colton's fingers again and then go to a new doctor and tell how the accident happened up on the fracking rig and how he'd put up with the pain for a few days but now he couldn't stand it. The idea was to get a new Oxy script. But he'd waited too long this time, gotten too tan. When he peeled the cast off his skin was moist and pale with that straight incision. It didn't look like any hand that had just been working.

"Fuck," he said. "Fuck a fucking duck."

He went out into the mud yard where the dogs were pacing past their filigreed porches. He started rubbing the orange dirt all over his arm, into the cut and onto his palm.

"Hey, let's just go find Ditro. I bet he'll front me a gram," I said. Ever since Natasha died, Ditro acted like he was scared of me.

Colton howled. His hand was the goose that laid golden eggs. He couldn't leave her yet.

"Last time I seen Ditro he didn't have shit," he said and he opened the trunk of his car and pulled out a sledgehammer. He glanced up at me then over to Luther then back to me.

"Right here in the middle," he said. "Just blam! One good smash."

He hauled the sledgehammer over to a tree stump and turned to look at me. The forest was busy, squirrels gathering nuts and woodpeckers drilling for grubs. I was holding a lukewarm backwash beer.

"Fucking idiots," Luther said and he walked away. The dogs all turned to watch him go.

I stepped up, swallowed my beer and set the bottle down. "How hard?" I said.

"Give it everything you've got."

The sun was warm on my back but it had been more than twelve hours since my last Oxy and I was starting to feel the sickness creeping in. I picked up the sledgehammer. It was so heavy I had to bend and stick my butt out to get a good enough angle to support it. I wondered if Luther was watching.

Colton's hand was splayed on the stump, his tan arm, tan fingertips, and pasty pale hand smeared with mud. I shifted my legs and focused my eyes on it. Behind me I could hear the dogs clanking their chains. I pictured them straining to get a better look.

"One," I said, "two, three."

I missed.

The hammer hit the mud and Colton screamed. "Fuck you!" Funny thing was that when I did really get him, he didn't say anything. The hammer hit his hand with a kind of wet smoosh that made my stomach turn. I let go as soon as it made contact and the hammer bounced to the side and landed in the pine scrub. Colton sat down heavy. His face was white and his eyes big. His hand was still pale and slick with mud but it was all crooked now, his pinky kicked back like it had an extra joint. There was only the sound of the dogs' chains and the squirrels cutting nuts and Colton's heavy breathing. He lay back.

"Come on," I said. "We gotta go. Where's your keys?"

Colton didn't move.

I looked around for Luther. The dogs watched me look, swiveling their heads, but Luther was not there.

"Colton, come on, we gotta go," I said.

I found the keys in his pocket and half dragged him to the passenger seat. He was heavy for how small he looked. Maybe it was just his oversized clothes that made him seem small, although if you asked him, I bet he thought they made him seem big. He didn't say a single thing the whole drive except for when I plugged his phone into the stereo and Metallica's ". . . And Justice for All" came on.

"Yes," he said then, "yes."

The doctor's office was in a half-empty strip mall between a Long John Silver's and an abandoned PayLess. From the looks of it, I wondered why Colton had even bothered to rebreak his hand, it seemed like he could've just said the word "pain" and gotten a new script. But apparently they were cracking down everywhere, even in shopping mall doctor's offices. The waiting room was all burnt-orange seat cushions with foam sticking out and dusty mustard curtains. A receptionist with spinach between her front teeth.

"My husband," I said to her, just as I had practiced. "He's in a lot of pain. He had an accident at work and I know it must be real bad because he usually never ever complains."

They kept him in the back a long time. I didn't know how long it was supposed to take but I started getting nervous. I kept looking down at my arms. My jean jacket was covering them but I still felt like the receptionist could see the marks. I didn't know if I was supposed to act worried about Colton but I did know I shouldn't act nervous. There was a woman across from me with an oxygen tank. When she pulled out a pack of Pall Malls, I bummed one.

"She won't let you smoke it in here," the woman said, cutting her eyes toward the receptionist.

I held the doors for her and when we were outside, she asked me to push her oxygen as far away from her as the tube would go. "It makes me nervous."

There were only five cars in the whole long parking lot. At the far end a kid was riding a skateboard. He kept steering it into the puddles where little birds were bathing. He would zoom through and they'd lift and swirl and dip down again.

We were back inside when Colton got through. He'd found his words. His arm was in a sling and he was hollering. "Fuck you all you cocksucking, motherfucking . . . My hand is fucking busted to shit and you won't do shit about it."

My stomach dropped. The receptionist was watching with an almost smile on her lips and the oxygen lady was shoving her glasses up on her nose to get a better look.

He whirled past me and out into the parking lot and I had to run to catch up.

"Colton, what happened?" I said.

"Fuuuck YOU!" he screamed.

I made it into the passenger side of the car just before he tore off. The hills were bright with changing leaves, gobs of orange and yellow across the mountainsides, and the sky a sheer and staggering blue.

He was driving with his left hand, swerving all over the place. We shimmied past the Pizza Hut where Mom used to take me once a month with my Book It coupons. Five book reports for one personal pan. By the end of every month, I'd get four pans.

"Let's go find Ditro," I said. It seemed it was the only thing I could say.

"Fuck you," Colton said. He didn't have a big range of vocabulary either.

"Come on," I said. "I bet he'll front me."

Colton turned and looked at me. "You *bet*. I need better than that. You just smashed my hand with a fucking sledgehammer."

HE PARKED IN the back corner of the Walmart parking lot.

"We'll split up, fan out," he said. "Look for receipts. Look for ones with high-dollar shit but keep any of 'em that's got stuff worth ten dollars or more."

"Then what?" I squinted over at him.

"Cash back," he said. "You go find the stuff, take it to the service counter with the receipt. Bingo. Cash back."

"Oh," I said. "Okay. Are you sure you're gonna be okay?" I nodded toward his sling.

"They gave my hand a shot of some kind of numbing shit. It's gonna wear the fuck off soon though. So get fucking cracking."

I took off toward the Garden Center, walking with my head down, staring at the pavement. I liked the straightforwardness of my task. It felt like something I could achieve, not like all the other big cloudy problems in my life. I'd been maybe permanently suspended from dancing at Southern X-Posure. I'd missed too many shifts without calling in. It didn't seem like you could exactly get fired from a strip club, but Raven had taken me completely off the schedule until I "got my shit together." I'd burned through my savings fast. I was shooting my Oxys by then but my script was gone and the pills were expensive. Dope was cheaper but the quality was never reliable and ever since Natasha died, I was worried.

The wind was blowing the trees along the edge of the lot and the flag in the yard across the street. A nice, strong ripple breeze. I saw a bit of white paper under a truck tire and I skipped toward it, smiling. This whole thing seemed magical and funny. Find a piece of paper, turn it into a different kind of paper, and turn that into Oxys. The world was a funny, magical place.

There was an insulated thermos on the receipt worth $11.60 and a pack of batteries, $7.99. Plus a bunch of other two- or three-dollar items.

"Colton!" I called, holding the receipt up above my head. I couldn't see him through all the vehicles though. The Walmart lot was full up. I kept having to dodge people with buggies and babies, keeping my eyes on the ground the whole time. I could feel the sick building in me, in my sweat and in my stomach, but finding the receipt had given me a little surge and I felt sure we'd get ourselves fixed up.

"Hey, miss, hey, did you lose something?"

I jerked my head up. There was a man with a goatee staring at me. "You alright, miss?"

"No," I said. "It's okay."

"'No'?" he said. "Or, 'it's okay'?"

"What?" I was rubbing the receipt between my fingers. My eyes darted away, looking for white paper.

"I said, are you alright?, and you said no." He was standing next to a blue pickup.

"Oh," I said, walking past him. "Alright."

There was something in among the leaves at the base of a light pole. I bent and grabbed it and when I stood up the man was right in close to me. I could smell the Skoal on his breath.

"I swear I know you from somewhere," he said. "You look real familiar."

I wondered if he'd seen me naked.

"You lose your shopping list, sweetie?" he asked.

I looked down. It was in fact a shopping list, not a receipt. I balled it up and threw it so it bounced off his chest.

"See ya," I said.

It turned out that the first receipt I found would be the only one for me that day. Colton found two but all together it only added up to thirty-seven dollars. We needed at least twice that much to get both of us better. If we added in the little stuff on the receipts it got us to just over fifty but Colton said you couldn't return every item on every receipt or they got suspicious.

"Go into the baby department and grab some pampers and formula," he said. "That shit always resells. I know a guy in Ronceverte who'll take it off us."

I did just like he told me and put the diapers and formula in a buggy and pushed it over to the automotive department.

"I already paid for this up front," I said to the guy behind the desk. "My husband's just out there getting the car looked at. I need to get back to my baby."

The man buzzed the door for me and I loaded it into Colton's trunk and we drove down to the river city. The Greenbrier was moving fast and smooth with a high current from all the upstream rain. It was late afternoon and the sunlight through the willows made me ache in a way I couldn't separate from the sick that was coming on strong by now. Colton had a little trashcan stashed behind the passenger seat. I vomited into it. I hadn't eaten anything all day. It felt like I was barfing up my heart. When it was over, I looked up and we were parked right across from the spot where Cam first kissed me, in the back seat of Mom's car, almost exactly two years before. The barfing made tears come out of my eyes but I wasn't crying.

"Let me have that," Colton said and he took the trashcan and handed me an empty Walmart bag.

The house Colton took me to was one of those big old white ones with front and back porches, three stories tall. There was a pit bull on the front steps and the man had to call him off before we could go in.

"We've got pampers and formula," Colton told the man and the man said go talk to Terry.

The house was set up like an indoor yard sale. There was a room for food stuff and another with lawnmowers and chainsaws. One room with men's clothing and another for women's. Everything had handmade price tags on it, a couple bucks cheaper than what it would cost at Walmart. Everything was set up neat and clean. Mom would've loved this place. She loved discovering things she didn't know she needed. Zucchini spiralizer, guillotine bagel slicer, doll-head toilet seat. Mom would've loved Colton's uncle's dog houses, too, all that intricate hand-cut wood. Before Cam, Mom had been my best friend and I always thought of the world through what she would like. Then Cam came in and I learned her music and her new language. And soon Cam was in on Mom's tastes, too. And then I spun out—Kandice, Colton, Mitcham, Jason Hicks. I had no idea if they liked kitsch or what kind of music. I had no idea what Colton liked besides Oxy.

The stairs creaked as Colton wandered up to the second floor. I was going to follow but I had to stop and barf. Every time, right after I retched, I'd feel better for a minute before it settled in again and I was standing there holding a bag of bile, strings of it sticking to my lips and teeth.

Colton came back down hollering. It was one of those grand type staircases, the kind a Southern belle would walk down in a hoopskirt, ready for a ball. "Fuck you," Colton yelled. "You cocksucking, motherfucking son of a whore."

The dog leapt up when we came out onto the porch.

"Ralph," the man called and he lay back down.

TERRY HAD ALL the pampers and formula he needed. He also didn't have any Oxy. We got back in the car. Colton tried to light a cigarette but started to barf. I handed him the trashcan. When he finished, he looked over at me, eyes all watery. "At least you can use the baby junk," he said.

I shook my head. Eva ate solid food now and Cam was getting her potty trained. I stared out the windshield at the river park. The sun was down below the ridge and the cold was settling in. I could feel goose bumps rising on my sweaty skin. Somewhere in there with the cold and the dark coming on and the images of Cam and Eva, happy up in Charleston without me, a corkscrew of hate started to mix with the dopesick. We just needed fifty, maybe a hundred bucks, and everything would be erased.

"I know where we can get some cash," I said. "Let me drive."

It was blue dark by the time we reached Kandice's. There were lights on in all the apartments except for hers. I still had a key even though it had been almost a year since I'd babysat. We used our cellphone lights to pick our way through a maze of plastic toys and dishes. I headed for the bedroom with the Willie Nelson poster and overflowing dresser. The bedroom where she taught me to dance. *There you go baby girl, that's good.*

"Hey, come on, hurry," he hissed.

I moved toward the closet. "Don't worry," I said, "I know her schedule at the club, she won't be home for hours yet."

I could've just taken fifty bucks. She probably wouldn't've even noticed. I could've just taken a hundred, a hundred and fifty. But I cleaned her out. At the time I thought I didn't know why, but now I know I was trying out the size of my greed. I was building toward something.

WE WENT STRAIGHT to Ballew's. On the road it had started to rain, but inside it was all warm and happy. Junie was serving her extra-generous shots. Mitcham was there, he hadn't been put away yet. The river was burbling down in the dark. And Ditro had black tar.

I bought us fresh rigs and we ran giggling through the rain to Colton's car. Colton had to shoot up in places like his foot or his crotch but I could still use the veins in my arms. We settled into the back seat and cooked up our shots. The taste came up over the back of my tongue and then the rush overwhelmed me. I was weeping, shining, leaping. It was like coming up from the bottom of the pool when your lungs are all empty. Pure relief that peaks so hard it shakes you. I watched the rain on the glass, the dark soft around us. Colton was sighing deeply beside me. And then blink! The Christmas star came on. It was this huge, twenty-foot-tall star that lit up on the side of the water tower on the hill above Render. It only ever came on in late December. I never saw it out of season but that night it must've fritzed. Life was a funny, magical thing.

"Hey look, Colton, look," I said but he'd nodded out.

I watched the light shine through the rain and felt its warmth spread in rings around me and it was gone then—that corkscrew of hate and everything dark I was ever capable of.

15 : CRASH N BASH

Sleet. That's always how I think of Huntington. Sleet and clouds so low you could reach up and touch them and the river always there, no matter which way you turn. We ended up staying in an abandoned house but it seemed like it was right in the middle of a regular neighborhood. That's how everything was in Huntington, all jumbled together: average cozy kind of houses and streetwalkers and grandmas and grandpas and college buildings and junkies and the best Chinese food I'd ever eaten, right there in the bottom floor of a skank-ass motel.

That's where we found Brandon, that day in December. Colton said Brandon always had a hookup. Ditro and Terry hadn't had anything for four days. Colton told me to stay in the car while he went up to Brandon's room, but I wandered into the lobby. The people who ran the motel spoke English but the woman who was cooking didn't. She gave me a bowl of something I didn't recognize but it smelled real good. I didn't even like eating anymore but I ate two bowls of it. Outside it was sleeting. Inside I was achy, my nose drip-drip-dripping. The windows that looked out on the parking lot and the river beyond were yellowed with nicotine.

Colton yelled at me for leaving the car and I told him to shut the fuck up. We weren't dating. He couldn't yell at me like that. Brandon said, "Spunky!" and I laid down in the back seat. Brandon could get us dope but the second half of the problem was, none of us had money. Both Colton and Brandon had people who owed them. We drove around. I lay in the back seat and looked at my phone. Looked at Cam's Instagram. Watched her TikTok videos. I hadn't seen her in almost two months but I knew from Instagram about her engagement ring and Eva's adoption paperwork.

I'd missed the last three Eva weekends. I couldn't get myself balanced enough. Mom wouldn't talk to me after I missed the first one. I still slept at home sometimes but I'd go in and out through the sunporch. Last time I saw Cam, she was buckling Eva into Ben's car and they were both singing the alphabet.

Shining, beautiful, competent Cam. The longer I went without seeing her in real life, the more my rage leaked from Ben to Cam. Flickers of it caught in my memories of her.

We didn't find anybody in Huntington who owed Colton or Brandon anything, but we did find this girl Brandon knew who liked to take photos and she had pharmaceutical speed from this fat friend of hers. Appetite suppressant. We all took some and went to an abandoned house. It reminded me of Natasha. Another big white house. Only this one was in the middle of Huntington of course. We went inside and Brandon and Colton started yelling. *Shit fuck motherfucker.* Somebody'd already got the copper wires out.

"Check upstairs," Brandon said.

The wires were gone from the whole house but the curtains weren't. Long, filmy white curtains. The speed started to kick in and I let the photo girl take pictures of me wrapped in the gauzy nylon. *Here comes the bride, all dressed in white.*

It was dark by then and we took more speed and made a fire in the backyard. I think it started forming in my mind that night but it wasn't a plan until the next morning. I saw the TikTok video that night though. Cam and Eva in matching *Frozen* nightgowns. Ben was taking them to Disney World, an engagement and adoption celebration.

If Ben hadn't made Cam promise never to let me in the condo I wouldn't've thought of it. I know that sounds exactly like the kind of stupid blaming thing a drug addict would say, but I think it's true. I think he put the idea in my head.

I woke up in that abandoned house in Huntington, curled in an afghan, a puddle of vomit beside my head. Outside the sleet had turned to rain and it was loud on the roof. I felt sicker than I ever had before but I had a plan.

I thought of the woman who had cooked the soup for me yesterday. Her face had said she didn't want to be in Huntington either. Maybe I should take her with me. I lay on the floor and watched the morning come on. I was surprised at how long morning and evening were in a house with no electricity. How slowly, slowly the light bled away and then inched back in again. How many different kinds of darkness and light.

My phone only had 5 percent. I put it on low battery mode and swiped through Cam's Instagram photos. Over her left shoulder, a stereo. Beside her right hip, a PlayStation. Just above Eva's head, a Blu-ray player.

If it had just been Colton and me, I wouldn't've tried. No matter what he said, I didn't believe Colton's experience. Up until two months ago he'd relied on prescriptions. But Brandon seemed more up to it. "Crash n bash" is what he said when I asked him.

"What?" It sounded too stupid to be real.

"All the alarms is set up with a timer, like thirty seconds, sixty seconds, you know, that way when you get home you go turn it off, right? So if you break through a door—crash! It don't set off the alarm right away. You search it out and bash! It won't send no signal after that."

The photo girl was still hanging around, taking pictures. I thought maybe there was vomit crusted on my lips.

"You know this place good? You been inside?" Brandon said.

I nodded.

"You know where the key code for the alarm's at?"

I shook my head.

"It's got a basement?"

"No."

We smoked cigarettes in Colton's car and plugged my phone in to charge. I flipped through Cam's photos again, squinting at the walls. Brandon leaned over the seat.

"Like a little remote-control type thingy," he said. "It'll be on the wall most likely."

I jerked the phone away. It came unplugged.

Colton was crumpled in the front seat. I wondered if he'd be able to drive. It was full morning now and there were so many hours of light for us to wait through until it got dark.

The photo girl was taking pictures from the outside of the car. I opened the door and asked her for some more of her fat friend's pills.

It turned out that the key pad was on the kitchen wall. In the photo where I found it, Cam was holding up a cake with cursive yellow frosting. HAPPY BIRTHDAY BEN! ♥

Once upon a time, she had held her hand on my belly and traced the branching veins. One hundred thousand miles, she said, more than four times around the earth. And under my skin, inside me, Eva's own circuitry—another map growing.

WE MADE IT to the Teays Valley exit and found a Rite Aid. Extra support pantyhose on sale, two for $14. Brandon stole four pairs even though we only needed three.

The hours between one and one stretched so long. Childhood long, like Christmas Eve or when I waited for Mom to wake from her nap and take me swimming. Hours big and roomy enough to live whole lives inside.

Colton and Brandon were sick and cagey. They turned music on, fought about what to pick, turned it off. Punched each other. Talked about each other's little dicks. They were just the kind of guys that scared me most in school. They weren't scary though. They were stupid.

BEN'S CAR WAS in the driveway. It freaked Brandon out but it didn't surprise me. Cam had said something once about how he always took Uber or Lyft, how he'd left his car at Yeager Airport one time and the door got dented.

We drove on past.

"You're *sure* nobody's home?" Brandon said.

"No," I said. "I mean, yes, I'm sure. No one's there. Disney World."

The temperature had dropped quickly and the rainy streets had turned to ice. We parked on the far side of the road and got out and the air was like a knife in my throat. The rain had frozen and coated everything, every tiny naked branch, every single blade of grass.

We crossed toward the condo. I remembered Cam in May on that sidewalk waiting in a NIN t-shirt. Brandon looked both ways and motioned for the pantyhose. With my face covered it was hard to see and hard to breathe but everything was warmer and sparklier. The nylons caught the streetlamp glow in the icicles and multiplied it times a thousand. I was stunned. Colton had to grab my hand to get me to move.

The next part, in my memory, always plays out too fast. Such a long day of waiting and then everything sped up. I was happy and excited. I know that sounds terrible but it's true. I was almost done with the heavy, slow, sleet, sick, vomiting days.

We circled around, squeezed through the bushes to the back patio. I wanted Brandon to have to break the sliding door, I wanted glittering glass, but he just wedged his EBT card between the handle and the frame and bent it until the lock popped. We stepped in, onto the living room carpet.

"Kitchen?" Brandon said and I pointed straight ahead.

We started to follow him but he shook his head. "Start unplugging," he said.

I knelt beside the stereo. It was very hard to see inside the pantyhose in the dark. I heard a bang in the kitchen and I jumped and then remembered, I guess that was the bash.

Brandon came back into the living room and he and Colton were each on one side of the TV when the light came on.

The light in the kitchen.

I saw Brandon's head jerk back and then he was gone, out the door. I swear, that fast. Colton right on his heels. The TV was sitting crooked in its stand. The condo was quiet now except for feet, moving across the kitchen tiles toward me. My heart was struggling in my throat. I watched the lighted doorway until Cam was there. Cam and Eva. I could only see outlines but I knew it was the two of them. Eva making little clucking sounds and then she was crying. She was crying and pointing at me.

"Who?" she cried.

I know it must've been fast, just a couple of seconds before Cam called for Ben, but time had turned long again.

"Who?" Eva cried and I lifted the pantyhose.

"Mommy?" her voiced keened high and I could see both of them perfectly now. Everything I ever loved. In their Elsa and Anna nightgowns, skinny elbows and pursed lips, their faces so radiant and howling.

16 | COUNT

I write between morning counts. We're not allowed to have lights on, but if I sit over by the bars, I can see enough to where I can scribble. This is the only time it's quiet in here, these few hours after the CO's done the 3 a.m. round and before the five o'clock count. I can think. Light leaks in just barely, mostly I'm writing by the feel of it. It really only lasts an hour, hour and a half max, before the sound of that first toilet flush rings down the housing unit and then it's over, one flush followed five minutes later by another and another and then voices and the COs and on and on and the noise just keeps boiling.

There's five regular counts a day, plus emergencies: 3 a.m.,
5 a.m., 4 p.m., 9 p.m. and midnight. Plus fog count. Four p.m.
count is a stand-up count so you stand and say your name,
like reminding yourself who you are day after day. Fog count
happens every couple of months when the clouds drop low
enough to where they can't see us. They cancel visitation and
lock us down.

I used to sleep through 3 a.m. count or try to anyhow.
I got used to the jangle of the CO's keys but some assholes
like Snedegger make a point of being loud. I couldn't imagine
voluntarily waking up that early but then I started working breakfast shift in the cafeteria and I started in on my
Biography of Dependency and I got to where I'd wake at three
and write until five. Actually, it was the other way around,
I started on my biography and then later I got stuck on the
breakfast shift.

I avoided the cafeteria work in here for as long as I could.
I knew what it would remind me of. At first, I had a good
job in the library, reshelving books and making photocopies
for the contract teachers. But the education director, Bostick,
hates me, and finally she found a way to fuck me over good.
There was this English teacher, Ms. Bennet, I really liked. She
was cute and kind of goth and sometimes I wonder if she's the
same teacher Cam had at community college. She was helping
me with my Biography of Dependency. To graduate from the
drug rehab program, we have to write fifty pages of our own
history. If we graduate, we're eligible for a sentence reduction.

In the group rehab meetings we're supposed to share what we're learning from writing about ourselves. We're supposed to reveal and repent, but sometimes it feels an awful lot like reveling, like those moments in the half-light at Ballew's, all of us tearing open our rawest hearts, comforted when somebody else is rottener inside than the rest of us. Of course, in rehab we don't have the substances to help get us there, but still we make it sometimes, even in that cinder block room under all that ugly drop-ceiling tile, every once in a while, when a girl gets started on her story, I'll see the flame light and rip along the wick that is *admit, admit, admit.*

Sometimes we share our stories back in the housing unit, too. There's this one girl, Garnet, who I like. She's sweet and she saves the insides of toilet paper rolls to curl her bangs. She tried to kill her husband in his sleep. Stabbed him in the heart with a corkscrew. She got the idea from watching *True Romance* with one of her johns. It didn't take me long to realize that living here in the housing unit is just about like spending time backstage at the club. Some of the girls you want to fuck, some of them you want to fight, but you're better off doing neither one because no matter which you choose, you're still gonna be stuck with them in a little concrete box.

Anyhow, Ms. Bennet, the English teacher, and I had a good rhythm going for a while. I made copies of the readings for her classes and typed up her notes and she helped me with my biography. She was a contract worker so she didn't have an office. She worked out of the library. I'd bring her coffee or something from the kitchen whenever I could. She circled my misspelled words and told me over and over again to *describe it more! I want to see, smell, hear!*

One day last June, I made a copy of an article that wasn't on Ms. Bennet's list. It was an essay I'd read when I was reshelving magazines. It was all about a woman teaching writing at a correctional facility. It showed how terrible the guards and staff were but how much of a difference the contractor workers could make. I wanted to share it with Ms. Bennet. I put a copy of the article in the stack with the copies she'd ordered and I went to lunch. I was gonna tell her about it when I got back, but she came in early and showed it to Bostick. It's not Ms. Bennet's fault, she thought it belonged to someone else, wanted to make sure it got to the right person. When Bostick looked at my list and saw no one had ordered it, she read it, or at least some of it, and she freaked out. Said I was trying to secretly communicate with Ms. Bennet, giving her an article that said disrespectful shit about correctional facilities. Blah-blah-blah. I lost my library job and got kicked out of the drug rehab, lost my chance at the sentence reduction.

Now I work in the cafeteria and shadows of Cam and Mom are there with me every day, Shania's "That Don't Impress Me Much" blaring across the kitchen while we mopped.

Except for the fact that I can't stop the memories, it's not a bad job really. The compound is quiet at five fifteen and the animals are all out. In the soft dark there's nothing but the fuzzy outline of the head and shoulders of the inmate in line in front of me, the jangle of the CO's keys, animal eyes in the wet grass, and the whispery limbs of the small trees. There's tame squirrels and rabbits and chipmunks and skunks, turkeys and groundhogs, and my favorite, a little doe who loves French toast. She smells when we're cooking it and comes to the back door, butting the screen with her head. By that time the sun's up a little and gadflies skim in the puddles by the oil trap. When the chow line slows, I take the leftovers. Me and Garnet head out back. She's from the city and before this, she'd never even seen half these kinds of animals. We lay the pan out on the pavement and stay as close as the doe will let us, watching the fake maple syrup drip from her lips.

I save up all the cute animal stories for Mom and Eva and Cam. Even though Cam hasn't come to visit, I know Eva will tell her. Eva talks to me about Cam (*Mama graded*, she says grinning, *Graduated*, Mom corrects), so I know it must go the other way, too. I work my way through the week toward visiting day like I'm climbing a rope, hand after hand, hours counted down to the visiting room. I stick stories away in my brain all day, some for Eva and for Cam, some for Mom, some for me.

Mom has these little sandwich bags with quarters divided into the right amounts for the vending machine snacks. She keeps them in her car for me. Well, for me and Eva and her. She has no other reason to keep bags of quarters with her. She comes here only for me. We sit in yellow plastic seats at orange Formica tables, and for this one hour, the visiting room is a warm pool that holds me and for this one hour it is right.

I'm not allowed back in the drug rehab program but for some reason, I keep working on this biography. Last week, they took us out to the highway to clean up trash. At the rest stop there was this tree. I'd never seen one carved quite like it, the initials overlapping, hearts covering every inch of bark. And none of it making any sense. Scars on scars. You couldn't read them but people kept putting them there. And any sense you might make had to happen in the blade.

Nobody is gonna see this except Garnet, she's still in rehab and sometimes we trade pages. I guess at first I kept writing because I was hoping I could still show it to Ms. Bennet but she doesn't even work here anymore. So maybe now it's just my private count, a way to say my own name over and over again until one morning when it can mean something new.

ACKNOWLEDGMENTS

Thank you to Bill, Kathy, Matt, Grant, Julia, and Carter.